The Baby and the Blueblood

The Baby and the Blueblood

AN EASTPORT BAY BILLIONAIRES NOVEL

TRU TAYLOR

Contents

About

THE BABY AND THE BLUEBLOOD

She's risen from the ashes of heartbreak...

As a single mom, I'm not looking for Prince Charming. The last time I fell for a handsome, sophisticated, wealthy guy, he left me at the worst possible time without a look backward or even a word of explanation.

He did leave me with a lovely parting gift though... which arrived nine months later.

With no way to reach him, I picked up the pieces of that shattered glass slipper and moved on. Now I'm running my own business—the Fairy Godmother Cleaning Agency. My hands—and all my hours—are more than full managing my employees (including my two hapless stepsisters) and keeping my four-year-old son happy, healthy, fed, and clothed.

It's not easy doing it all on my own, but I have zero interest in a new relationship. And who has the time? My high society clients expect their mansions to be sparkling—on schedule—come hell, high water, or hurricane.

So when a flu epidemic sweeps through my agency the day before the royal family of Aubernesse is to arrive in Eastport Bay, I put on a uniform and pick up the slack, working furiously to make sure their gorgeous vacation home is immaculate and ready for the elaborate ball they're planning to throw.

He's looking for the perfect fit...

I'm back in Eastport Bay for the first time in five years—and *not* exactly happy to be here. There's a reason I've stayed away so long.

The place lost its magic for me long ago—the night the only girl I've ever loved proved beyond a shadow of a doubt she didn't feel the same.

But this trip is non-negotiable, a matter of duty. I'm planning to fly in, attend the ridiculous ball my mother is so insistent upon, then get back to my life in Europe as quickly as possible.

That is until I arrive at the family estate early and catch the cleaning crew still at work.

And get a look at the woman beneath that coating of dust, ash, and spiderwebs...

Enjoy the story!

ONE
Overtime

You can't really grasp the full essence of the word "mortified" until you've stood face to face with the former *love of your life—covered head to toe in soot and cobwebs. – Cinda Brown*

I could hardly believe what I'd heard coming out of my stepsister's mouth.

"Both of them?" I gasped.

Olivia nodded at me from the receptionist's desk. "I guess the flu's going around."

The head of the cleaning crew I'd dispatched to 600 Bellevue Avenue this morning had just called and said two of her staff, Janice and Zoe, had started vomiting and were running high fevers. She'd sent them home.

It had been the right thing to do of course. The idea was to *sanitize* the clients' homes, not fill them with germs and viruses.

But with two fewer workers, there was no way the enormous mansion would be finished on time, and that wouldn't do. The royal family of Aubernesse would be arriving in Eastport Bay tomorrow for the America's Cup finals and expecting their stateside "summer cottage," as they called the twenty-four-thousand square foot home, to be sparkling and ready for the ball they were hosting next weekend.

Fantastic.

Flu season had the *worst* timing. Three other employees had already fallen ill this week, including my other stepsister, Traci, who'd called in this morning.

She rarely made an appearance at work anyway, so I suspected her Friday "illness" was more along the lines of Netflix-itis than influenza, but still the business was critically short staffed.

That made it a challenge to get the regular homes on our list cleaned, not to mention the mega-mansions.

This one, though, was non-negotiable.

The Wessex family was an excellent client. I couldn't afford to let them down.

"I'll have to go over and help them finish up," I sighed. "Looks like it's going to be a late night."

I studied Olivia in her designer clothes and shoes. She hadn't actually done any cleaning herself since we were teenagers and my father had made us all work—his daughter and his stepdaughters alike—in an effort to teach us the value of good, honest work.

But hey, some help was better than none. Olivia would no doubt gripe about putting on the serviceable company uniform, but she could at least do some dusting.

"Actually, an extra hand would be amazing if you don't have plans this evening," I prompted.

Olivia scratched her arm with one perfectly manicured finger. "You know, I'm not feeling so good myself. I think I'm developing a rash. Maybe I should go home before I infect anyone."

She stood and picked up her Chanel handbag.

"Skin rash is not a flu symptom."

"Oh." Olivia blinked. "Well, it must be something else then."

Biting the inside of my cheek, I drew a long breath. "Fine. If you're not feeling up to it, of course I won't make you go. But if you can manage it, could you at least stay here till closing and lock up? We're so short-staffed."

Olivia's eyes widened in horror. "What about AJ? You're not planning to leave him here with me, are you? I'm terrible with kids."

A shudder went through me at the thought of leaving my helpless four-year-old alone with Olivia. "No, of course not. I'll call Kristal. I'm sure she'll come and pick him up."

Olivia visibly relaxed and sat back down. The phone rang, and she turned to answer it. "Fairy Godmother Home Cleaning Service. How may we help you today?"

Back in the manager's office, AJ lifted his head and looked up as I entered.

"Hi Mommy! Look what I made."

He pushed a sheet of copier paper toward me so I could admire the drawing he'd created with the set of crayons I kept in my desk for him.

I walked over and stood beside him, resting one hand atop his silky brunette curls.

"Wow. That's a very exciting scene. Is it a knight fighting a dragon?"

"He's not a knight. He's a prince. But he's also a fighter. What's that called?"

He turned his little face up and stared at me with trusting brown eyes, certain I had the answer. Warmth saturated my heart, and I gave his button nose a light tap with one fingertip.

"I'm not sure. I think you'd still call him a prince. But a valiant one."

"What's valley-unt?"

"Valiant. It means brave, courageous, heroic."

"Oh. I like that. Yes. That's what he is. And he's protecting his family."

"Oh my—he is brave, then. And does he have a big family?"

I was endlessly fascinated by my son's intelligence and imagination. He was always begging me to tell him stories, but honestly, the ones he came up with were usually far better than anything I could imagine.

"No," AJ said. "A little one. He has a princess wife and a four-year-old boy. What's that called, Mommy? When a prince has a little boy?"

"The son of a prince is also a prince. I think. I'll have to check on that."

I wasn't a royal-watcher. Hopefully I didn't have my facts wrong.

"The big prince protects the little prince and the princess. He takes care of them. They do everything together," AJ informed me matter-of-factly.

A wistful twinge twisted through my belly. It wasn't the first time AJ had drawn a family of three or concocted fantasies about a heroic father figure. I knew he longed for a daddy to do things with him, but I was doing my best to fill both parental roles.

"It's a wonderful picture," I said. "You'll have to show it to Kristal when she gets here."

"She's coming here?" Excitement lit his eyes, but it was quickly replaced by suspicion. "You said we were going to go home and make pizza for supper."

"I know I did, buddy, but I have to stay and work some more. You remember Janice and Zoe?"

He nodded.

"Both of them are sick and had to go home early. Maria

and Anna are sick, too. So I have to go do the cleaning instead."

He pouted, resting one plump cheek on his hand. "Why can't the people clean their own houses?"

"Many of them work hard at their own jobs all day long and don't have time. And some of them have houses that are too big for them to clean all alone. It's a good thing for us that they do need some help because that's how we get money to pay for our house and food, right?"

He nodded reluctantly.

I brushed my fingers through his shiny curls. "I'm sorry, buddy. I know you're disappointed, but I don't have any choice. I'm sure Kristal would love to make pizza with you. And then you and I can make waffles tomorrow morning."

That seemed to cheer him a bit. He looked up. "Yoda waffles?"

"Yep. And Darth Vader too."

"Okay." He gave me the sweet smile that always turned my heart into goo.

"Good. Now you get your backpack all packed up and ready while I go change into a uniform, okay?"

"Will you be home in time to tuck me in?"

"I should be," I said. "Unless something very unexpected happens."

TWO

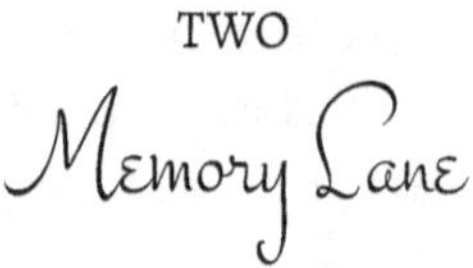

Alex

Thanks to the fair conditions, I touched down at Eastport Bay State Airport a few minutes earlier than expected.

The family's Rolls Royce Phantom sedan was there waiting for me. Patton, who was always on time, popped out of the front driver's side door when he spotted me.

"Your royal highness." Patton strode toward me, wearing a broad smile. "I hardly recognized you. You've gotten even taller. I think. If I hadn't spotted your Gulfstream landing, I might not have known it was you."

I clapped the old driver on the shoulder. "It has been a while, hasn't it? Good to see you, Patton. How's Iris? The kids?"

"Oh, all very good. They were excited to hear about your engagement. Congratulations."

My good mood at seeing Patton for the first time in nearly five years dimmed. "Thank you. It's not actually official yet, but it'll be a good match, I think."

Actually, my *parents* were the ones who thought so, and in my life, that was all that seemed to matter.

Patton took my bags and loaded them into the trunk. "I saw pictures on the internet."

He waggled his thick gray eyebrows, and his strong Rhode Island accent made the word sound like *pitch-urs.* "She's a pretty girl, Audrey deRamel. How'd you meet her?"

"We met once when we were kids, around eleven or twelve. I haven't seen her since then, but you're right, she has grown up to be a beautiful woman. And I hear she's nice."

The driver nodded, unsurprised, as he opened the car door for me. "You always were the good son. From what I see of your brother's behavior when he's in town, there won't be any arranged marriages in *his* future anytime soon."

I laughed. "I wouldn't be so sure. My parents are pretty keen to marry us *all* off sooner rather than later."

Patton climbed behind the wheel and started driving toward my family's Eastport Bay home. "Are they still planning to arrive this weekend?"

"They are," I said. "My father had an event to attend today, so they'll all be flying in together. I wanted to get here a bit early and... settle in."

In all honesty, I'd wanted to come alone ahead of the others so I'd have a chance to make peace with the place I hadn't seen in so many years. That, and I enjoyed flying myself when I got the chance.

"Well, they should easily make it before the storm then," Patton said. "Don't know if you've looked at the forecast, but it's moving up the East Coast and should make landfall around Thursday night or Friday morning. Hopefully you won't have to cancel that big party."

Yeah, that would be a real shame.

Out loud, I said, "These things usually peter out by the time they reach Rhode Island, don't they?"

"Usually," Patton agreed. "Of course, I remember Hurricane Bob in ninety-one. It was intense. Did some real damage to Block Island. Messed up the beaches here, too. You're right, though, usually these things downgrade to tropical storms before they get this far."

"Speaking of beaches... I'd like to take the long way home if you don't mind, along Atlantic Avenue. I haven't seen it in so long."

"Sure thing. No better scenery in the country."

Atlantic Avenue was part of Eastport Bay's famous Seven Mile Drive. Featuring views of Eastport Bay Harbor and the yacht club, the Eastport bridge, and a historic fort dating back to the Revolutionary War, the drive also passed by the childhood home of Jacqueline Bouvier Kennedy and the site of her wedding reception with President John F. Kennedy.

A little farther and the ocean came into full, glorious view. With its impressive seaside mansions, sandy coves, and rocky outcroppings, the Seven Mile Drive drew tourists to Eastport Bay year-round.

For me, it might as well have been named Memory Lane.

As the car meandered along the avenue's twists and turns, I rolled down my window to let in the cool onshore breeze and stared out at the gray-blue water, watching it crash repeatedly against the black shale, sandstone, and slate that made up the shoreline.

As always, the steady wind had drawn kite enthusiasts to the Stony Point State Park. The colorful beacons bobbed and weaved in the clear fall skies like dancing fairies.

I used to look forward to my family's annual stay in Eastport Bay. The place had held almost a magical allure for me when I was younger.

But in the past five years I'd excused myself from the annual New England pilgrimage, making alternate summer plans as far away from this place as possible.

When the car rounded a bend, the reason for my avoidance came into view. A crescent of coarse gray sand called Kingsley's Beach.

Well, it wasn't the fault of the place itself, but of what had transpired there.

The exclusive private beach club wasn't much to look at—a gray brick central pavilion flanked by two bathhouses and eighty or so cabanas where members could change and store their belongings for a day on the shore.

What I hadn't known as a child was that each of these simple cabanas cost more than fifty thousand dollars, provided you could even buy one.

They generally only became available when the last member of a family died, as they were passed down from generation to generation of Eastport Bay families bearing names like Drexel, Auchincloss, Slocum, Vanderbilt, and Astor. They'd prided themselves on the old Yankee simplicity of the surroundings, enjoyed membership not because it was worth the money, but because it *wasn't*, and they could afford to have it anyway.

Some of them visited Eastport Bay for only a few short weeks in summer, as my family did.

Others were year-round stalwarts of the Eastport Bay old guard, America's ruling class still presiding over one of the country's very first playgrounds of the rich and famous.

"Patton, pull over here, would you?"

The driver did as I requested. "It's off season," he said. "The club will be closed."

"I know. I just want to... look at something." I got out with a quick, "Be right back."

As Patton had warned, the club's buildings were closed, but I stepped onto the beach and walked toward the water.

Painful-sweet memories flooded my brain like the rising tide washing in. This place contained the most beautiful—and most excruciating—memories of my life.

Like seagulls swooping and pecking at a sandwich dropped in the sand, they came at me, taking sharp bites from my heart with each pass.

Cinda's long, blonde hair whipping in the sea breeze.

Her laughter carried on the wind.

Our tanned bare feet, leaving prints side by side in the damp sand.

Those prints washing away with the gentle surf, disappearing as if they'd never existed.

Running a hand through my hair, I tipped my head back and stared up at the clouds forming above.

What the hell am I doing here?

There was no point in this other than to torture myself. I'd seen far more beautiful views and spent time in places that put this one to shame—one of the privileges of being born into a wealthy royal family.

What had made this spot special was *her*. And she was gone. She hadn't wanted me. Without her, it was nothing but sad.

Maybe I'd wanted to prove to myself that none of it had been real, that the powerful feelings I associated with Eastport Bay had been nothing but an overgrown boy's flight of fancy.

But if comfort was what I'd been seeking, I certainly hadn't found it here today.

If duty didn't compel me to stay in town and receive my new almost-fiancée and her family next week, I'd ask Patton to drive me back to the airport.

Instead, I forced myself to leave the husks of old memories behind and slipped into the back seat without a word.

"Did you find what you were looking for, son?" Patton asked as he pulled back onto the road.

"No." I sighed. "It's gone. Let's go home."

THREE
Dust and Ashes

Cinda

The distance from my company's headquarters in Eastport Bay's business district to the Wessex mansion on Oceanview Avenue was only a few miles, but the drive always felt like crossing dimensions.

The quaint, Colonial feel of Main Street and its bright, busy wharf area gradually gave way to larger, more elegant structures and then the posh shops and cafes that marked the entrance to the most famous street in the "Village By The Sea."

Featuring views of Narragansett Bay and Block Island Sound, the entire three-mile length of Oceanview Avenue had been declared a National Historical Landmark.

Acres of immaculate landscaping, stone walls, large old-growth trees, and elegant brick and iron estate fencing surrounded massive Gilded Age mansions.

Built around the turn of the twentieth century by wealthy industrialists like the Vanderbilts and the Astor family, most of the magnificent homes had been donated to the Eastport Bay Preservation Society decades ago.

Now they were open as house-museums and drew tourists from around the world to this country's smallest state.

The newer, private homes, like the one owned by the Wessex family, tended to be set farther back from the road and secluded.

The crests of those mega mansions peeking over tall privacy hedges served to remind everyone—the tourists who walked up and down the sidewalks taking photos, and the workers, like me—of the distance between the "haves" and the "have nots."

I passed one mansion owned by Jack R. R. Bestia, the famous fantasy author, whose bestselling Onyx Throne series had been made into a wildly popular TV show.

His new next-door neighbor was the current heavyweight champion of the world, Sullivan Reece, though I'd heard the boxer was rarely in town because of his training and fight schedule.

I'd been meaning to reach out and offer my company's services and made a mental note to do that tomorrow.

A few houses down stood a massive stone mansion that had been subdivided into five large condominiums and was currently being rented out by the founders of a new software company that had recently gone global, making millionaires, if not billionaires, of all of them.

The locals had dubbed it "Billionaire Bachelor House," which I thought was kind of funny.

Reaching Palais du Soleil, as the Wessexes' European styled home was called, I pulled up to its ornate iron gates and punched in the security code, driving forward when they swung inward.

Parked in the circular drive in front of the house was the Fairy Godmother Home Cleaning Service van with its rosy-cheeked animated namesake painted on the side panels and rear doors.

I parked behind it and went through the mansion's tall wooden front door into the dramatic entry hall with its black and white marble flooring and direct view out to one of the home's back terraces and garden temple.

Katy was working in the library, wiping down the imported European wall paneling. She looked over her shoulder when I entered the room, sagging in relief and probably exhaustion.

"Oh thank goodness you're here," she said. "There was no way we were going to make it. I even made the girls turn off their music so they'd concentrate and work faster."

I gave her a sympathetic smile. "I'm sure they loved that. Where are they?"

"I've got Renata cleaning the chandelier crystals in the dining room, and Christina is working on the floor-to-ceiling windows in there. We've already changed the linens in the master suite and the six guest bedrooms, but they need to be vacuumed, and the fireplaces still need to be done. We haven't even started on the kitchen. All that china in the china room will need to be washed by hand, not to mention all those glass-front cabinets."

She sounded panicked, and I patted her arm.

"We're going to make it. I promise. I won't leave till it's done. I'll be in the kitchen if you need me."

"You're a saint," Katy called after me. "It's a good thing you're not one of those sit-in-your-office-on-your-tuckus kind of bosses."

"No way. Cleaning is my cardio," I joked and heard Katy's laughter echoing down the hallway.

Unfortunately, sitting in the office for some of the day was part of running a company, but I made a point of getting out and cleaning alongside my employees on a regular basis.

It was good for morale as well as giving me the opportunity to do a little quality control and remind myself of what they were dealing with every day out there in the trenches.

Not that the homes we serviced were unpleasant. On the contrary, most of them were pretty spectacular.

Back when I'd been a kid working for my father's cleaning company, most of his clients had been small businesses and modestly sized homes, owned by the working-class residents of Eastport Bay—like my family.

The only connection we'd ever had to the upper echelon was the contract Dad had signed the summer I turned twenty-four with the Singing Rock Beach Association, more commonly known as Kingsley's Beach.

In spite of the fact his company had done well, and he could easily have afforded to pay other workers to do it, he'd put me and my two younger stepsisters to work cleaning the cabanas and the pavilion, much to my stepmother's dismay.

"We should be facilitating friendships for my girls with the sons of the rich club members," she'd protested. "... not turning them into their servants."

"Good honest work never hurt anyone," my father had replied calmly.

Of course, my stepmother Julia claimed it was all that work that had sent my father to an early grave. That summer had been his last.

He'd died of a sudden heart attack, and Julia, who'd inherited his business but had no interest in actual work, had run it into the ground within only a few months, losing that lucrative contract and declaring bankruptcy.

It had taken me many years—and a lot of convincing of some of those same wealthy club members—to claw my way into some semblance of success with the Fairy Godmother business I'd started.

Instead of resurrecting the rather basic name of my dad's

company—Joseph's Housekeeping—I'd named it after my mother's favorite fairy tale, Cinderella.

No glass slippers for this girl. I chuckled to myself as I walked through the butler's pantry and into the china room off the kitchen.

Wow. Definitely going to be a long night.

Katy hadn't been kidding about the china. The place settings seemed endless, the cabinets holding them stretching up to the ceiling.

Just the glass fronts of the cabinets would take a couple hours to clean, and the number of windows and mirrors in the formally decorated home would require gallons of glass cleaner to polish and shine.

When the girls finished in the dining room, they took over for me on china duty while I cleaned out the fireplaces then went upstairs to vacuum and tackle the master bathroom.

Boy did the superrich enjoy their wood paneling. It stretched from floor to very high ceiling in the bathroom and even lined the outside of the tub surround.

After working for hours, I finally finished the upstairs. I checked my watch and realized AJ's bedtime was drawing near.

Shoot. It was late. I wasn't going to make it home in time to see him and read a story with him before he went to sleep.

I headed downstairs to check on my employees and to retrieve my purse with my phone inside so I could at least call and say goodnight.

On the way down the grand staircase, I pulled cobwebs from my hair and wiped my hands on my uniform, which now that I looked at it, was none too clean.

These old mansions tended to get very dusty when not in regular use.

I'd also splashed myself pretty well while cleaning the deep bathtub, so the dust and ash on my clothing had become mud in some spots.

Oh well, the only man I'd be spending time with tonight was Jim from The Office reruns, and he wasn't likely to complain. I was looking forward to putting on my coziest pjs and curling up in bed with the remote— *after* a very long and very hot shower of course.

The sound of the front door opening startled me. The shock multiplied exponentially when I heard a male voice.

A very rich, deep, cultured voice, with a distinct accent.

I froze on the stairs, my heart pounding like a trapped rabbit as the owner of that voice thanked someone for driving him and stepped into the entry hall.

He was tall, dark-haired, incredibly handsome. His fit body was encased in a perfectly tailored suit that looked like it had cost more than my two-bedroom house.

Though the last time I'd seen him he was wearing nothing but swim trunks and a swipe of zinc oxide on his nose, I recognized the man instantly.

Alex.

My brain screamed at my legs to turn around and run up the stairs like the mythical character in that fairy tale.

But I couldn't move. I was in shock. I'd never expected to see my first love again anywhere—and certainly not here.

What on earth was he doing, walking into the home of Aubernesse's ruling family like he owned the place?

Oh. No.

This couldn't be happening.

FOUR

Thank You for Your Business

Alex

"Honey, I'm home," I joked as I stepped through the front door—then immediately regretted it.

No one was expecting me to arrive until tomorrow. I'd probably just scared the wits out of the cleaning crew. If I took a broom handle to the kneecaps for arriving without warning, I'd deserve it.

No one was immediately in sight, but I knew they were still here. There were vehicles parked in the drive, and I smelled the homey scents of lemon cleaner and fresh laundry.

I took a few more steps into the foyer, wondering if I should call out again and identify myself before someone summoned the police.

And then I looked up.

Perched on the white marble stairs, at about the midway point, was one of the cleaning women. Her uniform was filthy, her shoulder-length blonde hair bedraggled.

Smeared on her forehead and nose was—what was that? Soot?

She must have been terrified because her eyes were wide, the whites standing out starkly against her smudged face.

"Hello," I said, holding up my hands palms forward to demonstrate my lack of criminal intent. "There's no need to be alarmed. I'm not actually an intruder. This is my house... or rather, my family's home. I'm Alexander Wessex."

The woman said nothing. Perhaps she didn't understand English? I repeated myself in Spanish, all the while drawing closer to the foot of the staircase.

With each step I took forward, she backed up a step.

"It's okay," I assured in a gentle voice. "I live here. I won't hurt you."

Her chest rose and fell in a rapid rhythm as she continued to stare. Finally, she spoke.

"You already did."

It was like I'd been struck on the back with a two by four. All the air left my lungs in a gust.

That voice. I'd know it anywhere.

And now, under all the smudges and grime, I recognized her face.

"Cinda? Is that you?"

"Hello Alex," she said, her stoic tone matching her grave expression.

A powerful rush of emotions made my legs weak. My heart was clawing its way up my windpipe, hindering my ability to breathe. I wasn't sure if I wanted to laugh or cry or both.

After all this time, after all the effort I'd put into trying to find her, here she was, standing right in front of me in my own house.

Frowning at me.

Right.

She left you, idiot. Stood you up. Didn't want to see you again.

My brain reminded my stupidly celebrating heart *why* Cinda and I hadn't stood face-to-face in almost five years.

While I had been ready to walk away from my country, my family, my duty, my entire *life* for her... she'd never even bothered to show up at our meeting spot the night before my family was due to leave the country.

I'd waited on that dock until well after midnight, a glittering ring in my pocket, my hopes and dreams sinking to the bottom of the bay like an anchor.

"How are you?" I asked to break the awkward silence.

"Good. I'm good." Cinda's voice quivered a bit, but her hands were steady.

I also noticed she wore no rings on those hands. Which didn't necessarily mean anything—she was doing housework—the company she worked for probably advised their employees not to wear jewelry on the job.

And it doesn't matter anyway, idiot. She didn't want you.

"It's... been a long time. You look good," I said.

She glanced down at herself and let out a humorless chuckle. "Figures that *this* is how I'd look when I saw you again."

Sighing deeply, she glanced away toward one wall and then up. Her unforgettable blue eyes returned to level with mine.

"And this is your house. You're a Wessex. I guess I understand now why you wouldn't tell me your last name all those years ago."

I took a step toward her, and Cinda jerked backward, losing her balance and sitting hard on the marble step behind her.

Moving cautiously, as if approaching a skittish animal, I joined her on the stairs, taking a seat a few steps below her.

"My parents forbade it. It was part of our security protocol when we were younger," I explained. "Back in Europe, there had been a few foiled kidnapping schemes against members of the royal family. My mother and father believed we'd be safer here in the States if no one knew our identities. That was why we didn't have cell phones either—so we couldn't be tracked. I've sometimes wished I'd broken the rules and told you who I was."

"Why?"

"In case you..." Self-respect wouldn't let me finish the sentence. "Never mind. Anyway, you still live in Eastport Bay. And you're still in the cleaning business."

Under all the grime, Cinda's skin blushed deeply. She stood. "Yes. And I'd better get back to work. We should be finished and out of your way very soon. Welcome back to Eastport Bay... Your Highness."

She practically ran down the stairs, heading for the corridor that led to the kitchen.

That was it? *Back to work?* She wasn't the least bit curious about what had happened in my life over the past five years?

Despite the way she'd abruptly ended our summer affair, I found myself afire with curiosity about what the last several years had been like for her.

Had she finished community college and gone on to get that business degree she'd always talked about pursuing? Had her stepsisters ever matured and started treating her more kindly?

Had she met someone special—someone she actually *loved*?

It didn't really matter. Our time together had clearly meant more to me than it had to her. The smart thing to do would be to let it go, to go about my business and let her get on with hers as she so clearly wanted to do.

I got up and followed her down the hall.

"Cinda. Wait. I'd like to speak with you for a minute."

Reaching the kitchen, she stopped and turned around.

There were three other women in the room, gathering their cleaning supplies, apparently preparing to leave.

"Is there something you'd like to discuss about the house?" Cinda asked in a business-like tone. "We pride ourselves on customer satisfaction."

Her face was tight, defiant, but there was a spark of panic in her eyes, and now her hands were shaking. She slipped them into the pockets of her apron.

Interesting. She wasn't as unaffected by seeing me again as she pretended to be.

The slip in her composure stoked the coals of my already burning curiosity.

What *had* happened all those years ago? How could I have been so wrong about her feelings for me?

How could months of being inseparable and crazy in love have turned into complete indifference so quickly?

I glanced at the other cleaning women, all of whom were now staring. This was not the time or the place to ask those questions.

Lowering my voice, I made an effort to keep the tone casual. "Maybe we could grab a cup of coffee—or dinner if you'd like—and catch up."

The spark of panic flared into a wildfire. Cinda turned away, grabbing her purse and a caddy filled with spray bottles and cleaning cloths. She didn't look at me as she delivered a reply in hasty, staccato rhythm.

"I'm not sure what the point of that would be. We're all done here. Thank you for your business. Enjoy your visit."

And she left, fleeing the house as if a swarm of murder hornets was in pursuit. The other women followed, casting bewildered glances at me before shutting the door.

Well, well, well. Whatever that was—it was *not* indifference.

"You can run but you can't hide," I said to the empty

room, pulling out my phone and strolling to the window overlooking the front drive.

On the side of the cleaning company's van, in a large font clearly visible from my vantage point, was a telephone number. I tapped it into my phone and hit the save button.

Cinda thought she was done with me.

She had no idea how wrong she was.

FIVE
Things Left Unsaid

Cinda

Kristal sat across from me at the restaurant on Monday, giving me her patented *Are you crazy?* look.

My long-time friend shoved her phone toward me. On the screen was a photo of Alexander Wessex, smiling in a suit and tie, his thick, dark hair windblown perfection, walking beside an equally handsome guy the caption identified as his brother Cameron.

"What am I missing here?" Kristal said. "He's gorgeous, single, six-foot-four, worth a zillion dollars, and oh, yeah, a literal *prince.* What is the problem?"

As I was trying to be "out of the office" as much as possible today, I'd asked Kristal to meet me for lunch at Nookie's Diner, one of our favorite places. I was buying, of course, to thank my friend for watching AJ Friday night.

The instant I'd told her who Alex, my long-lost love, really was, Kristal had pulled out her phone and done a search for him.

"That *is* the problem," I said, using my fingers to count off the reasons I couldn't have dinner, coffee, or even a *Tic Tac* with Alexander Wessex.

"He lives in a foreign country, he lied about his identity—well he didn't lie, but he hid the truth from me. He's not who I thought he was. And he's way out of my league. He's in your league. He's an aristocrat."

I left the biggest reason *off* the list. I was too terrified to even think it, much less say it aloud.

"I'm not an aristocrat. I don't even like society parties," Kristal said.

"You know what I mean. You grew up with people like that."

"And you grew up with *me*. Which means you should know that just because someone has money, it doesn't mean they're from a different planet."

Kristal Bianco and I had become friends in high school, bonding over our shared misery at the hands of our "wicked" stepmothers.

Not that long ago, Kristal's stepmother had forced her out of her family's mansion on Oceanview Avenue following her father's death and the foreclosure of the luxurious waterfront estate.

Kristal had spent a couple of weeks on my couch while looking for a new place to live and generally re-building her life from the ground up.

"I know *you're* normal," I said. "But the thing is, I don't know Alex—Alexander Wessex—at all. Not anymore. I don't know if I ever did."

"You know you loved him."

The statement reverberated through my chest, echoing in the emptiness like a lonely howl through a canyon.

There was no denying it. Not to my best friend anyway. Kristal had been there in the aftermath of both the biggest losses of my life—my father's fatal heart attack and Alex's disappearance immediately afterward.

Kristal had been away with her own family that summer and hadn't met Alex, but she'd rushed home for the funeral and dried way more than her fair share of tears during the next few months.

"I did. And I thought he loved me," I said. "But he left without even saying goodbye. I never heard from him again. His family probably has houses all over the world. For all I know he had a girl in every port, so to speak, and I meant nothing to him."

"If you meant nothing to him, I don't think he'd be asking you out and stalking you at work, trying to get you to talk to him."

Alex had called the office several times over the weekend, asking to speak to me. He'd called again this morning. I'd instructed both Olivia and the weekend answering service to simply say I was not available. He'd left his number and his name, identifying himself as simply "Alex."

I shook my head. "There's no point in seeing him. It was a long time ago, and there's a lot of water under the bridge. I've changed so much since then. I'm sure he has too."

"You never know. First loves are pretty powerful. And maybe you were *meant* to run into him yesterday. Lots of people reunite after spending time apart and live happily ever after."

"You do love your fairy tales, don't you?"

Kristal had seen more animated movies than any kid I'd ever met. Not only that, she'd recently found her real-life prince, Hunter, a guy we'd gone to high school with who'd apparently harbored a secret mad crush on her through all these years.

"Especially when they come true." Kristal took a sip from

her glass. "It *happens*. I'm living proof. All I'm saying is maybe you should just give it a chance. You work harder than anyone I've ever known, and you've taken some rough knocks in life. No one deserves for something good to happen more than you."

"Give *what* a chance? Do you really think a foreign monarch is interested in rekindling a relationship with someone he thinks is a maid?"

A sudden jolt of longing shocked me with its strength.

Even after all the years and all the resentment I'd built up against Alex over his desertion, it had only taken a glimpse of him to awaken feelings I'd thought were impossible for me to feel ever again.

I tamped them down again, stuffing them back into the lead-lined box where I'd stored them away once I understood he'd left without a backward glance.

"At *best* he wants to have another fling for old times' sake while he's in town," I told Kristal. "Anyway, I can't risk it. It's not just me now—I have AJ to think of."

And there, ladies and gentlemen, was the number one reason I couldn't chance even a brief conversation with the only man I'd ever loved.

"Exactly," Kristal said, oblivious to my fear. "It might be *good* for AJ to have a man around. Not to mention good for you. You shouldn't be alone, Cinda. You have too much love to give, and you deserve to *be* loved, and to have some fun for goodness sake. And you don't *have* to do it all by yourself. Case in point, at least half of Hunter's former housemates at the Billionaire Bachelor House hung on my every word whenever I mentioned you. Every one of them is cute as can be and filthy rich."

After losing her home, Kristal had upgraded from my couch to a guest suite at the mansion shared by Hunter and his six housemates, a group of friends and co-workers Hunter's brother had nicknamed the "Seven Dwarves."

The unconventional living arrangement had led to Hunter confessing his lifelong crush on Kristal and the two of them falling in love.

At my eye roll, she went on. "It's not the end of the world to count on someone, you know. Total independence is great in theory, but it's a lonely way to go through life. We all need someone."

"Not me. I'm fine on my own. AJ is fine."

Kristal dragged the tines of her fork through what was left of today's pie special at Nookie's—white chocolate banana cream—not looking at me.

After a long pause, she said, "You know... some people would say Alex has a right to know about his son."

"Kristal—"

Despite my warning tone, she persisted. "Think about it—you could get some financial help. He *should* be paying child support. You wouldn't have to struggle for money and work such long hours. You could spend more time with AJ."

Leaning forward, I lowered my voice. Though I loved Kristal like a sister, the sternness of it left no room for argument. "You will *not* tell him. You can't tell anyone. Ever."

"I know, I know. I would never—"

I reached over and gripped her hand on the tabletop.

"I mean it, Kristal. If Alex had showed up here, and he was just a regular guy, I *would* tell him. I would. But you understand my fears, don't you? He's a billionaire. He's a royal. His family has ruled over a European principality since 1304 for God's sake. He has power and influence I could never compete with. If he decided he wanted to sue for custody, I couldn't stop him. And if he were to take AJ back to Aubernesse for a visit, he might be able to keep him there, thousands of miles away from me. I might *lose my son*."

I had to swallow back an uprising of bile before continuing. "He's all I have—all that matters. I can't take the risk."

* * *

That night I sat on the edge of AJ's bed, reading aloud from the picture book he held, stealing glances at his long lashes, tiny cleft chin, and perfect profile.

So like his father's.

Since the first time I'd seen my child's face in the delivery room, it was obvious he resembled his father more than me.

When his downy baby hair had fallen out and was replaced by silky, dark locks, the resemblance was even more pronounced.

After seeing Alex again, I realized AJ didn't just resemble him—he was a perfect miniature version of the man who'd fathered him. I could not, under any circumstances, allow the two of them to be in the same place at the same time.

I was profoundly grateful my work and single-parenting schedule had kept me too busy to ever create a Facebook account or use any other form of social media.

As far as I knew, there were no pictures of AJ floating around in public anywhere.

All I had to do was be careful this week, keeping my son away from my office and out of public sight as much as possible. By next week, the Wessex ball would be over, Alex would leave town again, and life would go back to normal.

There was a buzz from my pocket. I reached into it, drawing out my phone.

Oh please don't let anyone else be too sick to work.

I did *not* need to work late this week. Kristal had come in clutch on Friday, but I didn't want to take advantage of my best friend's generous nature by asking her to babysit again so soon.

Seeing that AJ had already fallen asleep, I checked the screen.

My heart rate went from bedtime lullaby to thrash metal

rock concert in the space of an instant. The text wasn't from work.

It was from Alex.

How had he gotten my number? Never mind, he'd probably sweet-talked Olivia into giving him her "beloved" stepsister's personal contact information.

Either that or he'd greased a palm somewhere—he certainly had enough money to find out anything he wanted to.

That thought ratcheted my pulse even higher. Had he found out about AJ? Was that why he wanted to talk?

Again and again, I read the words on the screen.

Hi, it's Alex. Wonderful to see you last week. Sorry if I acted strangely. I was a bit overwhelmed. Would love the chance to chat. So many things left unsaid. Please call.

So many things left unsaid? What had he not said? What *was* there to say? My father had died of a massive heart attack, throwing my life into total disarray. When the dust had settled, Alex was gone.

He hadn't called or written or even wondered, apparently, why I hadn't shown up for our date that last night.

Maybe he knew why and just didn't care. All of this after promising to love me forever.

The two back-to-back losses had left me shattered. For a long time, I'd missed Alex and then been angry at myself for missing him. It had taken me months just to be able to function normally again.

Finally, I'd decided it was for the best that Alex had removed himself from my life when he had.

Someone who could so easily walk away from a relationship like the one we'd shared couldn't be trusted in the long term with my heart.

He *certainly* couldn't be trusted with my son.

I leaned over and kissed AJ's forehead, inhaling his soapy, clean little-boy smell, and pulled the covers more snugly against his chin before leaving the room.

Glancing back one more time, I flipped the switch to turn off the red airplane lamp on his bedside table.

"Good night, my little prince," I whispered.

Seeing his tiny form under the covers, fierce love gripped me. He *was* mine, and mine alone. And it would stay that way.

The two of us had made it this far without Alex's help, and we'd continue to survive without him.

Yes, it might be nice not to have to do it all alone, and of course little boys needed male role models to look up to.

But the risk was too high.

I couldn't take another loss of that magnitude, no matter what the potential gain might be.

SIX

Peace with the Past

Alex

It was good to have the family all together in one place again—it had been a while.

Janey had been far from home attending university in Boston, and Cam, being Cam, had been... everywhere.

My two siblings had excused themselves to get reacquainted with Eastport Bay, leaving me alone this morning in the mansion with Mum—unfortunately.

While I saw her on a regular basis back in Aubernesse and we got along well, she was in rare form today. The weather forecast had her in a furor.

"How *could* there be a hurricane during our visit? It just isn't right. I've put so much time and effort into planning this ball, and I want it to be perfect."

I chuckled at her indignation. "This *is* the middle of hurricane season. It runs from June first to the end of November."

"But fall in New England is *supposed* to be beautiful. That's why the deRamels wanted to visit Eastport Bay at this time. We've never had an issue with storms here in the summers."

"I don't know what to tell you. Unlucky break, I guess."

Or lucky, depending on your perspective.

As for me, I found myself siding with Team Hurricane.

It wasn't that I was planning to shirk my duty and back out of the royal wedding plans or anything. I would do what was expected of me, as always.

Audrey was an attractive girl, supposedly a nice person, and really, wasn't that the best one could expect? I'd already seen what came of falling head over heels for someone and giving away your heart.

It got broken.

So an arranged marriage to cement the understanding between our two countries made perfect sense. As my father, His Royal Highness, Henry Wessex, Prince of Aubernesse, always said, "Romance doesn't last, but family does."

It was just that I was dreading the whole public announcement, the ball-slash-engagement party, the whole "making it official" part. That would be the end of my life as I knew it and signal the beginning of a whole new level of royal duty.

I did feel bad for Mum, though. "Maybe the storm will fall apart before it even gets here," I said in an encouraging tone. "It happens all the time. It's still a good distance away. The Atlantic stays so cold up this far north that storms often downgrade by the time they reach Eastport Bay."

She looked somewhat mollified but still pouted. "I just don't see why it has to happen at all. I wanted the guests to be able to enjoy the gardens. And the fireworks—we *must* have the fireworks. It's all been planned. If it's windy and raining everyone will have to stay in the ballroom the whole time. Audrey's family will be disappointed."

"I'm sure they'll still be impressed. With all the flower arrangements and other decorations you've ordered, it'll be like being in a garden. I'll be happy to pick up a few sparklers if you like," I joked.

Mum didn't laugh. "That reminds me. I need to tell Francis to check on the permit from the fire department and ask Patton to get more ice. The deRamels will arrive on Thursday night, and I want everything to be completely ready."

"I'll pick up the ice. I've got to run an errand anyway." I kissed the top of her head and grabbed the car keys. "Don't worry. It'll all work out the way it's supposed to."

"You're a dear," Mum said and blew me a kiss.

Climbing behind the wheel of the Rolls, I drove toward downtown. My mother probably wouldn't have called me a "dear" if she'd had any idea where my *errand* would take me. I'd pick up the ice, but first I was going to the headquarters of Fairy Godmother Home Cleaning Service.

I'd called several times over the past few days, being informed each time that Ms. Brown was "not in at the moment" or "on the other line."

I did find out she was the owner of the agency, which gave me an unaccountable sense of pride.

Of course I'd had nothing to do with it, but Cinda had made a success of herself as I'd always known she would. I was happy for her.

Finally, after playing the VIP client card, I'd managed to wheedle a cell number out of the receptionist yesterday and sent Cinda a text last night.

She hadn't responded.

What was the matter with me? Clearly, she didn't want to talk.

But every time I told myself to let it go, I got a mental image of her eyes, that desperate, panicked look in them, and I picked up the phone again.

I had to find out if it was just my imagination or if there was actually still something there between us. And I was running out of time.

Once Audrey and her family arrived, I would be busy hosting them. I couldn't exactly go chasing around town after my old flame with my new fiancée in tow.

If I wanted to get any answers from Cinda about our past, this was my last chance.

The GPS led me to the agency's office with no problem, and I parked in a spot in front of the two-story office complex.

The Fairy Godmother agency was located on the second floor in a corner office. It was a small, functional space with a few desks out in the open and another smaller interior room with a closed door and drawn blinds—either an office or a storage room perhaps. A receptionist sat at a desk just inside the entrance.

A twenty-something woman in expensive clothing, she had her back turned to the door and appeared to be speaking on her cellphone while painting her fingernails. Slow day, I guessed.

"And then I told her, you should have slapped that skank for even speaking to him." The woman laughed loudly. "I know. Well, a girl's gotta do what a girl's gotta do—especially when it comes to bagging a rich guy, ya know?"

I cleared my throat.

The woman jolted around, eyes wide with surprise. "Gotta go. I'll call you back in a few minutes."

Ending her call, she gave me a bright smile, her eyes roving over me in apparent interest. "Hello. Can I help you?"

Her tone was more seductive than professional. I ignored it.

"Yes. I'm looking for Cinda Brown. I'm a client. I've called a few times trying to reach her. I was hoping I could catch her in."

Glancing behind the woman, I caught a flicker of movement. I couldn't be certain, but I thought the blinds on the interior office window had moved slightly.

"Oh. Yeah. Sure. Just a minute." The receptionist lifted the desk phone receiver and pressed a button, waited a minute and set it down. "She's not answering. Let me just go get her."

She stood and turned toward the small office but stopped when her cell phone chimed. Looking down at the screen, she appeared to read a message. Then she turned back to me.

"Um... actually she's not here. I guess she went out when I was on break or something. Can I tell her who stopped by, take a message maybe?"

My eyes went to the closed office door again. Cinda was in there. I knew she was.

Either she'd seen me park outside or she'd peeked through the blinds and had instructed her receptionist via text to get rid of me.

Frustration boiled up my spine, reaching my scalp and heating it until I felt my brains would fry.

I *needed* to talk to her, get some closure at long last. I couldn't be *this* close to her and not even see her.

For a moment, I had a wild impulse to charge past the receptionist and throw open the office door, force Cinda to face me or at least confirm my suspicion she was hiding from me.

And then you'd look like a lunatic. Not the impression you want to make—on her or *the American police.*

I rubbed my chin, breathing deeply to calm myself. "No thank you. I'll catch her another time."

The receptionist looked disappointed. "Are you sure you don't want to leave your name and number?" she asked in a hopeful tone.

"I'm sure. Have a good day."

I left the building, seething—not at Cinda—at myself. When would I get it through my thick skull?

It was a repeat of five years ago when I'd tried desperately to track her down, only to run into a roadblock at every turn.

I'd always suspected she'd asked her family to lie for her back then. Eastport Bay wasn't that large. The entire *state* had a population of less than a million. There was no way I would have failed to find her unless she hadn't wanted to be found.

When Cinda hadn't shown up for our rendezvous, my first thought had been that something had happened to her.

I'd been frantic, at a loss for where to turn. My parents had never allowed me to visit any of my friends' homes in Eastport Bay for security reasons, and obviously she'd never been to mine.

Cinda and I had only managed to see each other at the beach club. I had no idea where she lived.

So I'd called every Brown in the phone directory—and there were many—it was the second most common last name in the state of Rhode Island. Everyone I'd reached insisted there was no one named "Cinda" in their household.

One of them had to have been lying.

I'd searched social media for any trace of Cinda, thinking to reach her that way, but either she had no accounts, or they were under a different name.

Even after returning to Aubernesse, I had continued trying to track her down, but my efforts had all come up empty.

And now I knew why.

She had *wanted* a clean break. She'd known I was leaving the country the next day, and she'd chosen not to say goodbye, just as she was choosing not to see me now.

The feelings this time were a bit less raw, but the rejection still hurt. The months I'd spent with Cinda had been the happiest of my life. I'd never felt that way about someone before or since. At the time I would have bet everything I owned she had felt the same.

And I would have been wrong.

Returning to the mansion, I went to my suite and opened

my laptop. I needed to put Cinda out of my mind—for good. It wasn't fair to Audrey deRamel for me to still be this hung up on another woman.

That was no way to begin a marriage—arranged or not.

Maybe if I saw Cinda with another man, she wouldn't still feel so very *mine*. That was the excuse I gave myself for searching the social media sites for her. A few photos of her wrapped in the arms of a boyfriend or husband would go a long way.

But same as before, she had no presence on any of them. The only result a search engine query turned up this time was her place of business, which I already knew.

I slammed my laptop closed just as Cameron walked into my room.

"Wow. What did Apple ever do to you?" my brother quipped. He was dressed to go out—dark designer jeans, light cashmere sweater, brown Berluti leather boots.

"Nothing," I replied. "Just... frustrated."

"Don't worry. The weather will clear up. It wouldn't dare interfere with one of Alessia Wessex's fabulous society balls."

When I failed to laugh at his joke, Cam moved closer. "Hey, you okay?"

"I'm fine."

"No, you're not. You haven't had that sad sack look on your face since the last time we were all here and left Eastport Bay. This place makes you mopey."

"I saw her."

"Saw who? Audrey? I thought the deRamels weren't getting in until Thursday."

"Not her. The girl."

Cam's eyes bulged. "*The* girl? The one you were so messed up over?"

"That's the one." I told him about running into Cinda unexpectedly right here under our own roof.

"Incredible. How did she look?"

"Still beautiful. *More* beautiful actually."

"Excellent. When are you going to see her again?"

"Never, apparently. She's dodging my phone calls. She's not interested."

Cam made a scoffing sound. "Of course she's interested. You're a prince. Women are always interested in a prince."

"Not this one."

He looked truly perplexed. "Weird. It always works for me."

"It works for you a little *too* well. Anyway, it doesn't even matter. My engagement will become official on Saturday night. Might as well give it up and follow the family motto —'duty first.'"

Cam laughed. "You sound like Father. I prefer *my* motto —'me first.' Just tell Mum and Dad whatever it is they want to hear and then do what you want to do. That's my approach."

"Yeah, well, you're not first in line to the throne."

"And thank the gods for that." Cam grinned. "But being crown prince doesn't mean you can't have a life. You can still be with whatever woman you want to be with—even with the arranged marriage nonsense."

I gave him an affronted glare. "I'm not a cheater. Once I say my vows, I'm going to be faithful to Audrey."

Cam grinned. "Yes, but you haven't said them *yet*. You're not even officially engaged. And who knows, maybe you ran into Cinda for a reason."

"What reason could that be?"

"To give you a chance to make peace with your past—which you obviously haven't done, or you wouldn't be sitting there looking like such a mooncalf after one five-minute conversation with this woman. Listen, you've got a few more days left as a free man. I suggest you use them to see your long-lost love, find out that she's not the perfect paragon that your gilded memories have made her into but a normal, flawed woman like all the rest of them. Then you can put this whole thing behind you and step into your future without any baggage."

"When you put it that way it sounds like I'd be doing Audrey a favor by seeing Cinda again," I said.

His brother laughed. "There you go. Now you're seeing things my way."

"What if she won't see me? She's been avoiding me pretty effectively so far."

Cam raised a sardonic brow. "You've got boatloads of money and a royal title. You'll figure it out. So, are you going into Boston with me or will you make me go alone? I'm planning to grab some Italian food in the North End, and Janey told me about a sick new rooftop nightclub in the financial district. She's bringing some of her flatmates."

"Nah, you go ahead. I need to come up with a plan. I'm sure you won't be lonely for long."

"Never am. Good luck with it then."

"Thanks." I watched my younger brother leave, deciding Cam was right—I *had* to get over Cinda before I could move on with someone else—spend my *life* with someone else.

It was imperative.

Which meant drastic measures were called for.

SEVEN

Drastic Measures

Cinda

I returned from lunch, scanning the parking lot and sneaking into my own office like a thief. It seemed like the only way to avoid Alex.

I'd been stunned when I'd looked out the window this morning to see his Rolls Royce pulling into the parking lot of my office complex.

Well, he'd never been one to give up easily. The summer we'd met, I'd refused his first few invitations to walk on the beach with him, have lunch with him, knowing it was frowned upon to fraternize with the beach club guests.

But Alex had been so charming, so sweetly persistent, and God help me, so gorgeous, I'd finally given in.

We'd spent every day after that together, falling deeper and deeper in love all summer—until my father had died, and Alex had disappeared.

The office was empty when I got there, its door locked. Where was Olivia? I pulled my phone from my bag and checked the screen, remembering the device had chimed while I was driving.

Olivia: Sorry-had to leave a little early. Made an emergency hair appointment and Traci and I need to go shopping for formal wear. There's a prince in town! Mom's friend Cricket got the two of us invitations to a ball at his family's mansion on Saturday. Can you believe?

I could. My stepmother would do anything necessary to throw her two biological daughters into the path of rich men, including prevailing upon friends, relations, and virtual strangers if need be.

I was certain her attitude about them "marrying well" was the reason neither of my stepsisters had made use of their college degrees and instead relied upon me for a paycheck.

They swore they'd looked for jobs, and it was simply a tight market with nothing available. I feared it had more to do with the fact there was nowhere else they could get away with doing so little actual work without getting fired. I was sorely tempted at the moment.

It wasn't "a little early." It was only one o'clock.

I texted back.

Cinda: I need you here. You can shop after work.

There was no reply, so I called first Olivia and then Traci. Both calls went to voicemail.

Great. Now I was alone in the office for the rest of the day. I'd have to hide behind the closed blinds again, leaving the front desk unmanned.

The office phone rang, and I nearly picked it up on autopilot. Thankfully, I noticed the number on the caller ID readout first. It was Alex. Had to be—we didn't get many callers from foreign area codes.

Heart racing, I sat back in my chair and let the call go to the answering machine.

Once the light blinked indicating there was a message, I hit the playback button. It was Alex, all right, and he did *not* sound happy.

"This is Alexander Wessex. I've tried repeatedly to reach the management of this agency about an urgent matter. If I do not hear back from your manager, Cinda Brown, by the end of today, I will cancel my family's cleaning contract and take our business elsewhere."

His words were clipped and precise, his tone every bit as haughty and regal as you'd expect from a royal. "Furthermore, I will inform my friends and neighbors here about how unreliable Fairy Godmother Home Cleaning Services is and how unhappy I've been with your lack of communication with your clients. As we are hosting many of Eastport Bay's most influential residents at a formal ball this weekend, we'll have plenty of time to chat about such matters. Thank you and good day."

Good day indeed. He was blackmailing me.

Fuming, I lifted the receiver and hit the call-back button. Alex answered after one ring.

"That's a bit better," he said. "Thank you for returning my call at long last."

"If this is your idea of being 'charming' you'd better go back to prince-school. Your act needs some work."

He laughed. "Still as witty as I remember."

Not allowing myself to be swayed by his warm tone or the organic richness of his voice, I kept mine businesslike. "What do you want, Alex?"

"Don't worry. I'm not trying to strong arm you into a dinner date. I got the message loud and clear. This call is strictly professional. I need your services."

My shoulders, which had risen nearly to my earlobes with tension, settled a bit. "What can Fairy Godmother do for you?"

"I own a property on Block Island. The cottage hasn't

been used in quite some time and needs immediate attention. I'd like for you to take care of it for me."

"I see."

Block Island was a small island off Rhode Island's south coast, whose beaches and quaint New England charm made it a popular destination for summer and early fall visitors. It had only a tiny year-round residential population, and the hotels and many of the restaurants in the island's lone town closed for the off-season, shuttering their doors the last week of September.

I was surprised Alex's family would use their home there at this time of year, but maybe they wanted the seclusion and privacy. And who was I to ask questions? He was offering my agency more work.

It was certainly better than having the monarchy of Aubernesse trashing my company to all their tony Oceanview Avenue neighbors.

"How many square feet is the 'cottage?'" I asked.

That word had been used by some of Eastport Bay's most illustrious families over the years to describe waterfront mansions as big as a Walmart, so I knew better than to assume anything.

"Not big. A few thousand square feet. Four bedrooms. Six baths. Shouldn't take you long. And I'll be happy to pay a premium since I'm asking you to fit it in with your existing jobs with so little warning."

"Fine," I agreed. "I'll put it in the schedule for early next week."

"Oh, no. That won't do. We'll need it to be ready by this weekend. I need it done right away."

"There's a storm coming. If you weren't aware, Hurricane Beattie is moving up the coast and expected to make landfall here sometime on Thursday or early Friday. Even if it's downgraded to a tropical storm, the ferries won't be running."

"So do it tomorrow—before the storm arrives."

I rolled my eyes. *Rich people.* They really did think the world revolved around them.

"My crews are all busy tomorrow."

"I think you may have misunderstood me," Alex said calmly. "No crew. You. I want *you* to take care of it. No one else. There shouldn't be any heavy lifting involved, so you should be able to manage it alone."

I couldn't hold back my gasp. "*I'm* busy tomorrow, too."

"I realize you have a business to run. As I mentioned, I'll make it worth your while. How about a bonus to cover the inconvenience and late notice?"

Alex named an astronomical figure that made my jaw fall open. Now I was suspicious. No one needed their extra vacation home cleaned that badly. Or maybe he was just *that* rich and the vast sum was a mere pittance to him.

"Alex... you aren't by any chance planning to be on Block Island tomorrow, are you? Because I've already told you there's nothing—"

He chuckled. "I promise you'll arrive to an empty house. I have a noon meeting here in Eastport Bay tomorrow. It'll run well into the afternoon."

That reassured me. The last ferry to Block Island left the mainland at five p.m. Even if he did intend to go after his meeting, I'd be long gone by then. I could take the first ferry of the day at nine a.m. and be on the three p.m. return ferry at the latest. That would leave him no time to intercept me at the house—if that was indeed his intention.

And I needed the money.

I had to make this business work for AJ's sake. He was counting on me. To a lesser degree, so were Olivia and Traci. I could bank the money from this job to get us through the off-season and maybe even hire some extra hands for the busy season next summer.

Alex had literally made me an offer I couldn't refuse.

"Very well. I'll do it. But I want payment in full—*before* I get on that ferry."

"Of course. I'll have a check brought to your office this afternoon, or if you prefer, I'll wire the money directly to your bank account right now."

"A check will do fine." Just to be safe I added, "I'll be out of the office for much of the afternoon and my receptionist isn't in today, so just have the courier slide the envelope through the slot on the door."

There. All my bases were covered. I'd go to Block Island tomorrow, get the job done, and get back home as quickly as possible.

I could shore up my new business while successfully eluding Alex *and* keeping my secret.

Easy as Nookie's apple pie.

EIGHT

Slime Day

Cinda

The next morning, the skies were ominous.

A quick check of the day's forecast showed rain as well as increased winds, but the approaching hurricane seemed to be turning inland as it marched up the coast, so it looked like Rhode Island might be spared the brunt of the storm.

Since I wouldn't be seeing any clients today, I dressed in casual clothes—jeans and sneakers—and grabbed raincoats for myself and AJ as we left the house.

"I don't want you to go on the boat today," my young son whined from the back seat.

AJ wasn't a fan of storms, especially the kind that involved thunder and lightning. Some of his friends at the preschool had told him we were going to get a "hurricane that will blow your roof off," so he was extra spooked today.

The look on his face in the rearview mirror plucked at my heartstrings. I did my best to sound cheerful. "I'll be back this afternoon—maybe even before you get out of school."

"Will you pick me up?"

"You'll probably get to stay and play a little longer in the after-care program today, and Kristal might be picking you up."

She had offered just in case, and since I was desperate, I accepted, vowing Kristal and Hunter would have free house-cleaning for the next year. Kristal had laughed it off, but I was seriously going to arrange it.

AJ nodded, placated. "Matteo and Rick stay for after-care every day. I only stay sometimes. I like the trucks there."

I had thought we were over the rough patch, but when I walked AJ through the front door of his school, he burst into tears, wrapping his arms around my knees.

"I want to stay with you."

His favorite teacher Angelina rushed over and kneeled to help AJ out of his coat. "Hey buddy. I'm so glad to see you. Guess what we're going to do today?"

An adorable young woman in her early twenties, Angelina embodied all the qualities of her angelic name. She was only a part-time teacher's assistant, but I couldn't imagine anyone more suited to the job of teaching pre-school. If Angelina didn't make it her career, the three and four-year-olds of the world would definitely be missing out.

AJ sniffled and gave her a look of guarded interest, still clinging to me, his lips puckered in a pout. "What?"

"We're making *slime.*" The teacher waggled her eyebrows and gave him a wrinkle-nosed grin. "It's going to be really ooey-gooey and gross and *green.*"

AJ laughed.

"And for a slime-day snack, we'll have some gummy worms," she added.

"Can the gummy worms go in the slime?" he asked, completely intrigued now by Angelina's brilliant distraction tactic.

"They can, but those we can't eat. Because their wormy tummies will be filled with *slime.*"

As she said the last word, Angelina tickled AJ's belly. He released my legs and giggled.

I mouthed a silent "thank you" over his head as I bent over and hugged my son goodbye. Then he ran off toward a corner where several boys were moving rubber rocks around with yellow plastic diggers and dump trucks.

Stopping in place, he turned around and waved, "Bye Mommy!" before resuming his headlong dash for the truck corner.

Angelina still stood beside me, watching with a smile. "He'll be okay. Lots of the kids are on edge today because of the storm. They're like little barometers. Approaching storms and the full moon." She chuckled. "It's going to be an interesting day."

"Thank you again," I said. "Really. You're a miracle worker."

Angelina's cheeks pinkened in an instant blush. "Nah. I've just learned a few tricks since I've been here. It's you moms who are amazing."

"Well, you'll make a good one someday."

Her gaze swung from the children to me, and she blinked several times, blushing even more deeply. "I'm uh... going to be a nun."

"Really?" I probably shouldn't have said it in such a shocked tone, but I was... shocked.

Rhode Island *was* the most Catholic state in the nation, but I'd been under the impression most nuns were much older. Angelina seemed really young to have made a binding lifelong decision like that one.

And, not that this had anything to do with it, she was the kind of girl who could have her pick of men—sweet, beautiful, smart—the whole package. I also happened to know she came from money.

Angelina's mother owned one of the older Oceanview

Avenue mansions, which had been passed down through generations of her old-money family. I had heard Angelina's mom had enjoyed quite a reputation as a wild child in the 80's, but in recent years she'd been more of a recluse, rarely seen in public.

"Really," Angelina confirmed. "Right now, I'm considered a postulant, which lasts for several months, but I'm sure I'll go on to the novitiate phase where I'll be isolated with the other candidates for two years of discernment and then take my vows. It's what my mom has always wanted."

"I see." I nodded, a bit troubled. "And you too, I suppose."

The pre-school teacher hesitated a beat too long, looking away at the children again before answering. "Oh sure. Sure. I've always known it was going to be my life—as far back as I can remember. Mom used to buy me these miniature habits for my Halloween costumes."

When I looked into my own memory, I remembered wanting to be an ice skater, a singer, an archeologist. I couldn't imagine a little girl dreaming of growing up and becoming a nun, but it wasn't really my business.

"Well, it's a worthy occupation. The kids will miss you when you go into full-time religious service."

Angelina's expression fell. "I'll miss them too. But some nuns teach in parochial schools. I'm hoping someday to do that—when my religious order says it's time."

"Speaking of time... I'd better get going. I need to catch the nine a.m. ferry out of Point Judith."

"Hope you brought along some Dramamine," Angelina said, holding her stomach and feigning motion sickness. "The water's probably choppy as heck today."

I laughed. "I've got an iron stomach. See you later. Have a good day."

"You too, Miss Brown."

NINE

Luxury Waterfront Accommodations

Cinda

I lied.

Well, I'd thought I was telling the truth at the time, but my "iron stomach" turned out to be made of something far more malleable and prone to nausea.

Though I'd never had an issue on the ferry before, the waters of the Block Island Sound were putting on a rock-and-roll show during the hour and a half trip from the port at Pt. Judith to downtown Old Harbor on Block Island.

There were a few moments I truly feared I'd lose what little breakfast I'd had time to eat this morning.

As I debarked along with a surprisingly small number of other passengers, the ferry's captain gave me a friendly smile. "Have a nice long weekend and stay safe."

"Oh, I'm not staying over. I'm heading back home today."

His thick gray brows creased in concern. "The meteorologist at Right Weather is saying it's gonna be some pretty rough seas come afternoon."

"Those weren't rough seas?"

He chuckled. "It gets much worse, believe me. If you're

planning to head back to the mainland today, best catch one of the earlier runs. If the wind picks up too much, they'll cancel us for safety's sake."

"Do you think I'll be okay catching the three p.m.?"

The man looked up and around, as if the answer might be written in the gathering clouds. "Most likely. Two p.m. would be a safer bet though."

"Okay, thank you."

I hurried down the gangway and started looking for a taxi. I'd been planning to walk to the address Alex had given me, but now I felt the time pressure more keenly.

Several cabs were waiting near the terminal, and I climbed into the back of one, giving the driver the address of the Wessex cottage.

There was no traffic to speak of. Though fall was normally a beautiful time to be in New England, it was well past peak tourist season here on the island.

Many of the restaurants in town and all the hotels we passed displayed signs that read: "Closed for the season. Thank you for your business."

One was painted with a palm tree motif and said, "Gone to Florida."

Once I'd spent a day on the island with Kristal. We'd eaten lunch at a charming inn were our waiter had explained the inns and restaurants on Block Island frequently hired seasonal workers from western Europe and even Russia and Australia. The young workers would spend the summer here and then travel down south to work during the winter months.

I wondered briefly what the Wessexes planned to do during their off-season visit to their home here—play Scrabble?

Maybe that was what they wanted, peace and quiet and privacy. They'd have it in abundance at this location.

"You sure are dedicated to your job," the driver said,

smiling at me in the rearview mirror. "I saw your carry-all there. You a maid?"

I smiled back at him. "Something like that. I've got a very *demanding* client who just couldn't wait to have his toilets scrubbed."

I couldn't wait to deposit the obscene check someone had dropped off in my office's mail slot yesterday afternoon. It was the only thing making me feel marginally better about this entire ridiculous escapade.

"Well, I hope it don't take you long—not if you plan on going back today," the cabbie said.

"Oh, I do. On the three o'clock ferry if not the two. I have a little boy. I need to get home this evening. It's just a cottage," I assured him.

The Wessex house was about two and a half miles out from the town center, high atop Mohegan Bluffs on a six-acre plot of land with sweeping views of the ocean. As the car pulled down the drive and I got a look at the classic New England wood-shingled structure itself, my heart sank in dismay.

The "cottage" was huge.

It had to be at least five thousand square feet. It would take me forever to get the place cleaned alone. Well, I was getting on that afternoon ferry no matter what. I'd get done what I could get done, and if Mr. Alexander Wessex wanted to dock my pay for the unfinished job, he could just try it.

Thanking the cab driver, I paid for the ride and asked him to be back at 1:30 to take me to the ferry terminal unless he heard otherwise from me before then. I climbed the stairs to the home's wraparound porch and used the key that had been delivered along with my paycheck to open the front door.

The interior of the house was beautiful, with plentiful windows admitting natural light and overlooking the sensational water views.

White slip-covered furniture and honey-toned wood floors grounded the classic beach house décor, but the tasteful art and modern kitchen with its professional grade appliances reminded me this was the vacation home of an immensely wealthy family.

Case in point, a spectacular transparent baby grand sat in front of one ocean-facing window wall. I recognized it as a Bluthner lucid piano.

Owning one was a fantasy for most pianists. They were constructed of reinforced Lucite strong enough to support a small SUV but as fragile looking as Cinderella's crystal slipper.

The instrument was at once ultra-modern and traditional, an unexpected contemporary touch in the classic interior.

It was obvious the piano—and the whole house—hadn't been used in a long time. While perfectly neat, it was stale and dusty. I had my work cut out for me. Setting down my caddy of cleaning supplies, I took off my jacket and went to work.

As I moved from room to room, dusting and cleaning floors and changing sheets, the rain increased steadily. Its pattering on the roof and windows served as a constant reminder I needed to keep up my pace if I wanted to make that early ferry home.

By one-thirty, I was basically finished. There were a few baseboards I hadn't gotten to, but I'd done my best in the time I had. Gathering my things, I locked the door and stood on the porch waiting for the taxi to return.

It pulled into the driveway right on time, and I ran to it, climbing into the back seat, smiling at the driver. "Thank you so much for remembering."

He didn't return my smile. "I didn't forget, but I have some bad news for you."

"What is it?"

"The ferry has shut down service. All the other cab drivers went home to prepare for the storm. I'd be at my own house if

I hadn't promised to come back for you. Is there somewhere else I can take you? Maybe you've got a friend who lives here on the island?"

I shook my head. "Are you absolutely certain the ferries aren't running? The captain told me there would at least be a two p.m. run. I have to get back to the mainland today."

"I can take you to the docks if you like, let you see for yourself."

"Would you mind terribly? That way I can get a look at the hotels too and see if any of them are still open. I don't know anyone I could stay with."

The driver made his way down the steeply declining road toward the town center. It was deserted when we reached it. Rain lashed across the street in waves, sheets of it blowing sideways in the high winds.

All the hotels were dark and obviously closed. As he'd said, there was a sign outside the ferry terminal announcing service had been suspended. My heart dropped, and my mind scrambled for what to do next.

"Do you happen to know anyone who rents out rooms?" I asked the driver.

He turned around, sympathy evident on his face. "I'm afraid I don't. I'd invite you to stay with my family, but we've got four kids in a three-bedroom house. We don't have a guest room or even a pull-out sofa. What about the house you were cleaning? It's pretty big. Maybe they've got an extra room tonight?"

"Oh, I couldn't stay there. I..." My words drifted into silence as I considered it.

The house *was* empty. None of the Wessexes would be coming over to the island with the ferry service cancelled. And I had the key. I could spend the night there, wash the sheets afterward, clean the bathroom again. It made sense.

Besides, it was Alex's fault I was stuck here in the first

place. He *owed* me a free stay in luxury waterfront accommodations.

"Okay, you're right. Take me back there please. And I'm so sorry I made you get out in this awful weather for nothing. Your wife must be eager to have you home."

"Oh yeah. She's gonna hand me a honey-do list as soon as I walk in the door. It'll just be a different kind of workday. That is, if we don't lose power. You see any candles and matches up there in that big house?"

"I didn't run across any matches, but there are some candles. I'm sure they must have matches or a candle lighter there somewhere in a kitchen drawer or something."

He fished a cigarette lighter out of the car's center console and handed it back to me. "Just in case. Give me a call after the storm, and I'll take you back to the ferry—no charge."

"You're too kind. I couldn't accept that. This is your job. But I will call you tomorrow when the storm ends."

"Hate to tell you this, but it's not gonna be tomorrow. Don't know if you've ever ridden out a hurricane or tropical storm here on the island, but those ferries aren't gonna be running until at least Friday."

Two days? Here?

My ire with Alexander Wessex was growing by the minute. "Okay, well thank you. See you soon."

Pulling up the hood of my rain jacket, I got out of the back seat and made a dash for the porch.

The wind at this point was so strong I felt like it was actively fighting me, trying to prevent me from getting into the house.

It had been hours since I'd checked the weather forecast.

As soon as I got inside, I'd do that, gather up the candles, and then call Kristal and AJ and let them know what was going on—namely that I wouldn't be coming home for a couple of days.

TEN

So Close and Still So Far

Alex—Earlier that day

Taxiing my jet from the Block Island airport's single runway to the tarmac, I worked to calm my thundering heart and steady my shaking hands.

That had been by far the scariest flight of my life, and I'd made many.

I probably should have listened to the air traffic controller who'd advised me not to fly today.

The Gulfstream—not a light aircraft—had been buffeted by high winds, and the rain and clouds had gotten so bad I'd had to rely solely on my instrumentation for much of the flight.

There were a few moments when I'd started to wonder if poor Cameron might wind up as heir to the throne after all.

But I made it. I'm here.

That was all that mattered now. And very soon I'd finally have what I'd been craving since I'd first laid eyes on Cinda again—time with her.

Uninterrupted time to talk, to listen, to finally find out what happened that night close to five years ago.

Once I had some answers, maybe I'd *finally* be able to move on and forget about her.

Rain pelted me as I sprinted from the plane to the terminal building. The storm that had appeared to be weakening and turning inland had shifted east again in the past few hours and was continuing to plow up the coast, picking up speed once more.

Though it had been downgraded from a Category 4 hurricane to a 2, it was still no slouch in the storm department. Winds had been measured at ninety-six miles per hour, and the eye of it was somewhere in the area of Virginia Beach right now.

At the rate it was moving, the brunt of it would reach Rhode Island in a few short hours.

That forecast had been the determining factor in my decision to make the perilous flight over from Eastport Bay. I couldn't leave Cinda alone over here with a hurricane about to hit.

If something happened to her, I'd never be able to live with myself, especially as it was my fault she was here in the first place.

Naturally, I hadn't told my parents about my impromptu travel plans. For one thing, the deRamels were supposed to arrive tomorrow.

For another, they'd blow a gasket over the idea of me flying in conditions like these. And they'd demand to know why on earth I'd even want to do something so stupid.

I wasn't sure how to answer that. I didn't really know.

The Block Island airport had only a skeleton staff working. I spoke briefly with the guy on duty, Dave, who told me I was either brave or crazy or both for making the flight.

"I'll say this for you—you're a hell of a pilot. And that's a hell of a plane. Be a shame to see it damaged. I'll taxi it into the hanger for you. It'll fare better in there when the worst of the storm hits."

"Thank you. That would be fantastic." Then I thought about it. "Are you sure you wouldn't rather I do it? It's pretty nasty out there."

He brushed it off. "Nah. It's just water at this point. It's the wind that'll be a bitch pretty soon. You'd better get on to your house before the rough stuff starts. Someone's picking you up, right?"

"Actually I was planning to take a taxi."

Dave's thick, blond eyebrows pulled together, and his lips drew back in a *that's not going to happen* expression.

"They've all gone home for the day to batten down the hatches. Listen, I'd give you a ride, but somebody's gotta stay here and keep an eye on all those planes parked outside. I'm the only one here."

"Of course. No problem. I'll just walk."

That was easier said than done. I felt like I was in a wind tunnel machine or maybe one of those foolhardy weather presenters on TV who stands out in a battering storm while advising everyone else to stay indoors.

At times I had to lean my full body weight against the wind to stay upright. Raindrops hit my face and bare hands in stinging zaps, and my clothes were soaked within seconds.

The walk was only a little over two miles, but it took me a good hour to reach the house. Once I did, I dragged myself onto the covered porch and sat for a moment in a deep wicker chair, catching my breath.

Examining my sopping clothing and water-pruned hands, I laughed. This was not exactly how I'd pictured greeting Cinda.

Any hopes of dazzling her with my *princely good looks* were out the window.

After a few minutes I got up and went to the front door,

nerves percolating under my skin. I tried to open it, but it was locked.

Had Cinda locked herself inside for security? Probably not necessary out here on the island, especially off-season with so few people around, but I was glad she was being cautious.

I knocked. Waited. Knocked again.

Going to a window, I pressed my forehead against it and peered between the shutters. The lights were off, and there was no movement inside. Walking around to the back deck, I did the same thing.

The parts of the house I could see from here looked freshly cleaned. The wood floors and kitchen countertops shined.

Okay, so she *had* been here. Had she finished and left already?

Bollocks. My whole plan would be shot if she'd already gotten on a ferry and gone home.

Bracing myself for the pelting rain, I jogged down the back porch steps and squatted to reach underneath them for the spare key. With my fingertips, I located the small box screwed to the underside of the top step. I slid it open and extracted the key, walked back up the steps, and let myself inside.

Sure enough, the place was sparkling and fresh-smelling.

And empty. I'd missed her.

So close and yet so far. Fate seemed to be conspiring against me. All the excitement drained away, replaced by a sickening sense of dejection.

Well, there was nothing to be done for it tonight. I'd go upstairs, grab a shower to dispel the bone-deep chill that had overtaken me, hope there was something warm and comfortable to wear left in one of the drawers or closets, then rummage around in the pantry for some supper.

Not the evening I had planned.

I was also less than thrilled about riding out the storm here alone. It would have been the perfect time for Cinda and I to hash out our past, fill each other in on what had transpired during our time apart, and maybe even find some closure for that "summer fling" I'd never quite managed to recover from.

Unfortunately, I'd sorely misjudged her speed-cleaning abilities.

Feeling thoroughly sorry for myself, I trudged up the stairs toward the master bedroom. Though my brother and sister used the house on occasion, it was technically mine. I'd bought it during my last visit to Rhode Island.

The night Cinda had stood me up, the plan had been to surprise her by whisking her away on a mystery boat ride, arrive here on Block Island, and show her the new house I'd bought for the two of us to stay in whenever we visited the States.

I'd assumed she'd want to visit frequently to see the family and friends she would undoubtedly miss after moving to Aubernesse with me.

That plan had obviously not worked out, but I'd held onto the cottage for my siblings' sake. They said they enjoyed having a place to go and get away from our parents and the life of a royal for a bit.

No doubt Cam had also used it to impress the scores of young women who flocked around him everywhere he went.

Yep, this house had probably seen plenty of action. Regrettably, I had been party to none of it.

Dropping my wet clothes in a heap on the bedroom floor, I turned the shower on as hot as it would go and stepped under the scalding spray.

ELEVEN

World's Unluckiest House Maid

Cinda

Letting myself into the sturdy shingled house with the key, I struggled to push the door closed behind me again. The wind was like a living thing, straining against me at every turn.

I finally managed to click it closed and turned the lock, breathing out a sigh of relief. At least I had a warm, dry place to spend the night.

Might as well make myself at home.

Carefully, I drew off my rain jacket, making an effort to keep it from spraying water droplets in an arc around me.

And that was when I noticed the floor was already wet. I had mopped it earlier in the day, but I *knew* it had dried by the time I'd left.

How could it...

Spinning back toward the door, I stared at the lock. I *had* locked it behind me when I'd left, right? I nodded, certain I had.

There was a doggie door though. Had some animal, desperate to escape the storm, let itself inside?

When I turned back around, my pulse whirred in my ears.

My eyes scanned the dark kitchen, living area, and staircase. Flipping on the light, I braced myself to see a furry creature dart across my field of vision.

There was nothing.

"Here kitty kitty," I called softly, fervently hoping I was dealing with a domesticated animal and not something dangerous.

Like a raccoon.

Or a rat.

It was well-known that Block Island had a population of Norway rats, their hardy ancestors arriving on the island centuries ago with the first ships.

Maybe it was a dog who'd gotten spooked by the storm and slipped his leash?

Shivering in dread, I managed to whistle a few notes, an exercise in optimism.

"Here, boy. Come here. It's okay."

Okay, definitely not a dog.

A cat might hide from me, but I hadn't met a dog yet that wouldn't respond in *some* way to the call of a human. Unless maybe it was rabid.

Oh Lord, please don't let there be a rabid animal in here.

And then my mind leapt to an even more frightening scenario.

Or a human.

My heart went ice cold at the thought. Glancing behind me once more, I determined the doggie door was far too small to allow a person to crawl through. Just in case, I removed my shoes and tiptoed into the kitchen, withdrawing a butcher knife from the wooden block on the countertop.

I had never stabbed anyone or any*thing* in my life, but the sharp blade in my hand did make me feel more secure.

Brandishing it like a ninja, I moved through the first floor of the house, alert to every sound and potential movement.

When I reached the bottom of the staircase, I did hear something. A soft bump.

Could have been the wind blowing something against the outside of the house, but I thought it had come from upstairs.

Now I was worried.

Glancing at the back door, I considered just leaving. But the weather was so incredibly bad out. I had no car and couldn't ask Jorge to come back and get me again. No doubt he was home with his family now, preparing his own house for the storm's full assault.

Besides, I had nowhere else to go. It would be silly to flee this perfectly good, dry, comfortable home for the sake of what? A squirrel?

Still clutching the knife, I crept up the stairs one by one, wincing when one of them creaked under foot.

Really? This was a home owned by billionaires. Didn't they fix those sorts of things right away?

I went quickly to the second-floor landing and began moving from bedroom to bedroom. Finally, when I was nearly to the primary bedroom, I heard a sound.

It sounded like... rushing water.

Of course, by now the whole world seemed like it was made of rushing water, but this sound was distinct from the driving rains outside. At least I thought it was. Maybe it was my imagination.

Gently, I pushed open the bedroom door. At the foot of the king-sized bed lay a pile of sopping wet clothing. The door to the attached bathroom stood open, and the light was on.

Someone was in the house.

And apparently naked.

Did someone break in to take a *shower*? Well, whatever they'd come for and no matter *how* good their hygiene, they weren't going to get a crack at the world's unluckiest housemaid.

I turned around and headed for the door, scrambling to get my phone from my purse to call 9-1-1.

"Cinda?"

At the sound of my name, I whirled around. There, standing in the doorway between the master bath and the bedroom, was Alex.

He was bare except for the towel clutched around his waist. His hair was wet.

Water droplets decorated his chest and shoulders—wide, *muscular* chest and shoulders—which were underpinned by a set of abs the likes of which I had only ever seen featured on the front of men's health and fitness magazines.

Alex held the towel closed with one hand. With the other he shielded his groin area.

What— did he think I was going to kick him there? Actually, that thought sounded rather appealing at the moment.

Something flashing in my peripheral vision made me turn my head. Oh, I was holding the butcher knife up like the villain in a slasher movie. I lowered my hand and smirked.

"Really? *That's* what you chose to protect?" I said. "Where did your heart and neck rank on the list of priorities, I wonder?"

He shrugged. "I'm a guy. I'm rather attached. Once upon a time, *you* were rather fond of..."

"Shut up," I commanded.

Ripping my eyes from the breath-stealing vision, I spun away again, flushing hot with embarrassment.

"What are you doing here?" I demanded in a harsh voice, shouting back over my shoulder.

Nerves pinged all over my body. I was no longer afraid for my life but no less discombobulated than if an intruder had invaded.

"It *is* my house," came Alex's sensible answer.

"Yes, but you're not supposed to be here today. You *told*

me you had a meeting at noon in Eastport Bay. You said it would take several hours. And there were no afternoon ferries coming over—I checked to make sure. You lied."

"I didn't lie. I did have a meeting, and I didn't take a ferry. I flew."

Shock had me spinning back around to face him. "In this weather? Are you crazy? Wait—you have a plane?"

Alex had the nerve to smile at me. "And a pilot's license."

"You could have mentioned that when we spoke yesterday."

"You never asked. In fact, you haven't asked anything about me. You haven't let me say more than a few words to you since the other day. *That's* what I'm doing here. We need to talk, Cinda."

"No, we don't. And put on some clothes—*please.*"

Alex had a plane—of course he did. And he'd *planned* this. Getting me out here to clean his island beach house had been a ruse. He'd just wanted to trap me.

And it had worked.

Well, I'd show him. I *would* call Jorge and ask him to pick me up. I'd *find* someone with a room to let overnight if I had to knock at every door on Block Island and beg. I'd sleep under a bridge if I had to.

Well, maybe that was a bit drastic. My son needed me. I owed it to him to keep myself safe.

Charging from the room, I dug my phone out of my purse, dialed the number Jorge had given me, and stepped out onto the porch as it rang.

TWELVE
Winds of Fate

Alex

My heart pumped madly as I threw on a pair of jeans and a t-shirt I'd found in a bureau drawer.

She's here. In this house. Right now.

I hadn't missed her. The storm must have shut down ferry service, stranding Cinda on the island. I'd never been more thankful for foul weather in my life.

And I'd never been more nervous.

This was my chance—the only one I was likely to get. I would *finally* get some answers after all these years.

Padding down the stairs barefoot, I looked around. Where was she?

Not in the kitchen, not in the living room. I moved through all the downstairs rooms, my panic increasing with each step. The bloody fool hadn't gone out in this storm, had she?

There had been no car in the driveway when I'd arrived, and I'd already been informed the cabs weren't running because of the approaching hurricane. There was no way she'd try to walk to town in this.

Except that *I'd* walked. When you wanted something badly enough, you'd do just about anything, no matter how stupid, to get it. And what Cinda apparently wanted more than anything was to avoid me.

I was going to find out why.

Intending to head out into the storm myself, I yanked the back door open—and came face to face with Cinda. She was on the covered porch, phone in hand. The overhang normally would have provided some degree of protection, but today the wind was blowing the rain sideways, drenching her hair and clothing.

She didn't seem to notice. The expression she wore was a mixture of hopelessness and fury. She appeared to be on the verge of tears.

"He's not answering." Her tone was infused with frustration. "I can't believe this."

"Who's not answering? Who were you trying to call?"

So she *did* have a man in her life. I was shocked at the amount of malignant sludge that confirmation sent pulsing through my veins.

"Never mind."

She sounded as grumpy as she looked and took a few steps toward the staircase leading down to the waterlogged sidewalk. "You wasted your time and risked your life for no reason flying out here because I'm not staying."

"Where are you going?"

"Anywhere but here."

"That's insane," I said. "It's not safe for you to go out in this."

"It's not safe for me to stay either. I'm not exactly sure why you did this, but for once in your pampered royal life, you're *not* going to get what you want."

Gripping the handrail to keep from slipping, Cinda gingerly made her way down the stairs. I worried for her every step of the way. Everything inside of me wanted to snatch her up and carry her back indoors where it was safe and dry.

But I'd already learned forcing my will didn't work with Cinda. All I could do was hope common sense would prevail. Or a miracle would occur.

Just as she reached the last step, there was a deafening crack. One of the large trees close to the house had dropped a limb. It landed heavily across the walk and part of the driveway.

Maybe fate *wasn't* against me after all.

Twigs and leaves were picked up and flung about in the high wind. Cinda held up a hand to protect her face, frozen on the bottom step. She glanced around at the darkening sky, the thrashing branches and shrubs, the debris carried through the air outside.

"Please... come back inside," I yelled over the wind. "I don't want you to get hurt."

She whipped her head back to look at me, wearing an accusatory glare that seemed to say, *Yeah right.*

What was that about? If anyone had hurt anyone in this equation, *she* was the one who'd hurt *me*. She was the one who'd stood *me* up.

With a harrumph, Cinda reversed direction, climbed the stairs, and charged past me back into the house.

"Fine," she spat. "It's not safe to leave. But don't think this means we're going to roast marshmallows and sing Kumbaya."

I followed her into the house, closing the door securely behind us, awash in relief. "I don't even know what that is, and if you'll remember, my singing voice is marginal at best."

Turning around, I looked at Cinda, who was now standing in the center of the kitchen. Dripping from the rain, she looked like a baleful cat who'd been forced into a bath, edgy and skittish, ready to either claw me or run away at the slightest provocation.

I truly didn't understand her hostility. And it was a bit insulting she found venturing out into a hurricane preferable to staying inside with me.

Was it possible I'd done something to offend her all those years ago without realizing it, and *that* was why she hadn't shown up on the night I'd intended to propose?

For the life of me I couldn't think of what it might be. In my memory of those days, our relationship had been perfect—right up until the end.

"So..." I said, rocking back and forth on my feet, unsure of what to say or do now that I'd gotten my wish and had Cinda stranded here with me. She certainly wasn't in the mood to listen at the moment or divulge any secrets of her own.

She let out a sigh. "I guess I'm staying here until the storm is over." Her tone turned businesslike. "Do you have a radio so we can listen for updates or warnings?"

"I think there might be one in the basement storage area. Let me go check." I started in the direction of the stairs and then stopped. "If you'd like to change into something dry, there are probably some women's clothes that would fit you upstairs in the second bedroom on the right."

Cinda raised a brow in a way that made me feel scolded but also made me want to laugh.

"They're my *sister's*," I explained. "She and my brother use this house sometimes when they're stateside. Jane might have left something you could change into. She's about your size."

I couldn't be sure, but it seemed Cinda's expression relaxed a fraction. "I guess that *would* be more comfortable than staying in these all night."

Crossing her arms over her chest, she asked, "Where will you be while I change?"

Now I did laugh—just a little. "Downstairs finding the radio. And then in here, rummaging around for something to eat. You didn't happen to see any five-star prepared meals in the pantry or refrigerator when you were cleaning, did you?"

Cinda shook her head. "All that's in the fridge is some mustard, a stick of butter, and a jar of minced garlic. I did spot some canned soup in the pantry along with some other non-perishable stuff."

"It'll have to do. I'm famished—and I don't think we're going to find any takeout available in this weather," I said. "You go ahead and get dried off. I'll make some dinner for us."

"I can cook my own food," she snapped, the hostility returning in full.

I held two hands up in the classic surrender pose. "Fine. Suit yourself."

As Cinda started back up the stairs, I added, "If there's someone you need to notify about your change in plans, you might want to do it right away. Once the brunt of the storm hits, we're likely to lose cell service."

She nodded and marched solemnly upstairs. Despite Cinda's obvious bad mood, I couldn't help the surge of hopefulness in my heart. I had to fight the urge to whistle as I set to work making a dinner I *hoped* she'd relent and eat with me—pasta with a surprisingly appealing-looking jarred clam sauce. I also found some garlic bread sticks in the freezer which I planned to heat in the oven.

Overhead, I heard the bedroom door close and then the low, indistinct murmur of Cinda talking to someone on the phone.

Again, something that felt very much like jealousy twisted through my chest.

It doesn't matter, I told myself. *Whoever he is, he's not here. I am.*

And I had something I never expected to have—time alone with Cinda.

I planned to make it count.

THIRTEEN
Fool Me Once

Cinda

The reception to the mainland was a bit sketchy, but I was relieved to hear AJ's voice and to hear him sound so cheerful.

I'd been afraid Kristal might tell me he'd freaked out when she showed up at the school instead of me this afternoon. But when I told Kristal what was going on, she told me not to worry, that he'd been all smiles and had proudly showed off the jar of slime he'd made.

Now he was bubbling with enthusiasm describing it to me.

"It has three worms in it. One of them is purple, one is orange, and one is red. And Miss Angelina says I can play with them but not eat them. We had worms and dirt for our snack today, but the dirt wasn't really dirt. It was pudding and Oreo crumbs. Can we make that at home sometime? I asked Kristal if we can make it here, but she says we can't go out and get the in-credients until the storm is over."

"Ingredients," I corrected gently. "And if you don't get to make it with Kristal, then we'll make worms and dirt for dessert when I get back." I took a deep breath before the next part. "Listen, you're going to stay at Kristal's place for tonight, okay? Mommy has to stay on Block Island because they closed down the boats a little too early. But I'm fine, and you're going to be fine, too. Kristal told me she got some awesome movies for you two to watch."

"I know," AJ said. "Her house is so big it has a movie theater in it. We're going to have popcorn too. She said the house is built like a castle. The wind can't bother a house like this one."

I sent up a silent prayer of gratitude for my brilliant best friend, who once again had come in clutch.

"That's true. The houses on her street are like big old dinosaurs. They don't even notice the rain and wind."

"We're going to *watch* dinosaurs!" AJ said in a tone that indicated he thought I might have magical mind-reading powers. "Kris-thal got us the *Good Dinosaur* movie."

"That sounds awesome. Well, I love you, and I'll see you very soon. Be a good boy and don't stay up too late watching dinosaurs, okay?"

"Okay Mommy. I love you too. Want to talk to Kris-thal again?"

"Yes please. Night-night little bear."

Kristal's voice came back on the phone. "I wasn't sure he was ready for Jurassic Park, so I went with the animated one. We have a generator, so even if the power goes out, we're good to go."

"It's perfect. You're a genius and the best friend anyone has ever had. Thank you so much. I'm upping your free year of house cleaning to a lifetime membership, by the way."

She laughed. "Not necessary. It's no big deal. You know I love that kid—and animated movies. Hunter isn't quite as into watching them with me." Her voice lowered to a conspiratorial whisper. "So… how's it going with the baby daddy?"

The term made me cringe. "Ugh. Don't call him that. And

nothing is going *anywhere*. We're stuck here on the island until the storm ends. That's all."

"I don't know... you've seen those romantic comedies. The guy and the girl can't stand each other, but then they get stranded together, and one thing leads to another..."

"This is real life, not the movies. And you know better than anyone where letting one thing lead to another got me. I'm not making that mistake again—with Alex or anyone."

"Okay. Okay," Kristal said. "But it *is* kind of the perfect time to talk about things. Maybe he was just immature back then and not ready for a commitment. You've grown up a lot since then. He probably has too."

"We will not be talking about *things*. We're just going to get through the storm and go back to our lives."

"Really? You think that's realistic? You're going to make small talk all day and night for two days?"

"If necessary. Maybe we won't talk at all. I dusted a whole bookshelf full of books when I got here. I might just hole up here in this room and read until the storm passes. But no matter what happens, we will *not* be having any heart-to-heart chats," I insisted.

"Okay then. I guess you know best. It's not like I have any great insights on second-chance romances to offer." Kristal's tone oozed with sarcasm. "Be safe."

"You too. And thanks again."

I hung up, feeling better. AJ was safe and happy. I would be home with him soon. And what I'd told Kristal was true. I could handle this. I was sure of it.

Yes, the only man I'd ever loved was downstairs at this very moment, looking even more gorgeous than he'd been when we'd first met.

Yes, he'd fathered a child he knew nothing about. And yes, we were trapped together in a house for a day or two.

But after all the hardships I'd endured over the past few

years, after all the things I'd accomplished on my own, this was nothing.

If I could run a business, raise a child alone, and fix my own leaking toilet, then surely making small talk with my ex for a couple of days would be a cinch.

If I was ever tempted, all I had to do was remember the way I'd felt in those days after my father died when Alex was nowhere to be found and hadn't bothered with a phone call or even a letter. Nothing he could say could possibly excuse that.

And I would keep in mind the old adage that went, "Fool me once, shame on you. Fool me twice, shame on *me*."

Alex might have been the kind of man who made smart women stupid, but I didn't intend to be anyone's fool *ever* again.

FOURTEEN
While You Were Sleeping

Alex

I'm an absolute fool for this woman.

That was the thought pounding through my brain as Cinda and I sat together at the kitchen island, eating in silence.

To my surprise, she had agreed to eat the meal I'd prepared. And judging from the speed at which she was inhaling it, she was enjoying it—or maybe she was just really, really hungry.

She was makeup-free, her rain-drenched hair air drying, dressed in a cotton pajama set she'd said was the only clothing she could find in Janey's room.

It was the furthest thing from sexy—shapeless, covered in silly cartoon sheep—and the only thing I could think was that I'd never seen a more beautiful woman in my entire life.

I'd always loved everything about the way Cinda looked. From the moment I'd first seen her on the beach, carrying a tray of empty mixed drink glasses and crumpled juice boxes, I'd been captivated by her long, straight hair, her bright blue eyes, the sound of her voice, even the way she walked and the way she threw her head back when she laughed.

Time had made her even more beautiful, the years sculpting her face with a kind hand, though her skin looked as soft and fresh as it had at twenty-four.

I couldn't stop myself from sneaking peeks at her between bites. She, on the other hand, would barely look at me. I had a lot of work to do if I was going to warm her up enough to move beyond small talk and discuss the main event—our non-breakup.

Throughout the meal, I attempted to get conversation started, asking about her family, her friends, what she liked to do in her free time.

That question at least got a smirk out of her. "Free time? What's that?"

"So you really work all the time? No social life?"

My tone was disbelieving, but I couldn't help it. A woman like her had to be inundated with requests for dates. She was everything men wanted—beautiful, smart, kind.

When she didn't answer, I asked the question I'd been dying to know the answer to since running into her again. "Isn't there someone special in your life? Someone you spend time with?"

Cinda put her fork down and finally looked directly at me. "We're not going to talk about this, Alex."

"Why not? It's a simple question. Is there a guy in your life?" I shrugged. "A simple yes or no will do."

After hesitating a moment, she answered. "Yes. There is someone in my life—someone very special. I spend as much time with him as possible. Happy?"

I was not happy. Not at all. But I acted like the information didn't bother me. "Thank you. That wasn't so hard, was it?"

I should have stopped there, but I couldn't help myself. I had to know. "Any plans to get married?"

"No Alex, I don't plan to get married. Ever. How about you? There's no Mrs. Wessex, I take it?"

"Only my mother," I quipped, electing to leave out the fact that I'd be officially engaged in a matter of days.

But back to the more important matter at hand—whoever this "special" guy in her life was, he was obviously missing whatever mysterious quality it took to win the heart of the unmovable Miss Brown.

Just as she had with me, she'd deemed Mr. New Guy unworthy of a long-term commitment. She wasn't in love with him.

That thought gave me a twinge of perverse satisfaction.

Though she hadn't finished her food, Cinda slid off her stool and removed her plate from the counter. I was afraid that would be it, that she'd retreat to her room upstairs, and this lame, superficial conversation would be the last one we'd ever have.

I'd have to go back to my life, marry someone I didn't love or even know really while still wondering about what had happened to the only girl I *had* ever loved.

I had to do something.

As she rinsed her dish and placed it into the dishwasher, I spoke to her back.

"You know, while I was downstairs getting the radio, I noticed several bottles of wine in the cellar. Why don't I go down and grab one? We could open it and see if maybe there's a good movie on... or watch some Seinfeld reruns to pass the time."

Cinda had introduced me to the old television show the summer we'd met, and it had quickly become my all-time favorite. I now owned the DVD's of every season and knew the episodes by heart.

"I don't drink," she said flatly, seeming to have no memory of our shared obsession for the show.

Turning around, she came to the opposite side of the island counter and faced me with piercing, accusatory eyes. "Listen, I realize you're bored. You're used to a glamorous life and having women fall at your feet everywhere you go."

She lifted a hand and gestured around us. "And a windswept house with an ocean view might be the perfect setting for romance—*if* you were stranded here with someone else. But just so we're clear, there is not going to be a replay of what happened between us five years ago. My company's services are not *that* comprehensive."

With that she strutted toward the living room, grabbed a book off the shelf, and marched up the stairs. "Thanks for dinner," she called down before I heard the slamming of her door.

Well, that went splendidly.

Maybe I'd open one of those bottles for myself. I wasn't a frequent drinker either, but drowning my sorrows sounded rather appealing at the moment.

I got up and rinsed off my own plate. This woman was one tough nut to crack. But the storm was far from over, and it was bound to be a long night. We had time.

Unfortunately, she was up there, and I was down here, a situation I had no idea how to remedy.

Flipping on the radio, I turned up the volume, finding there was still reception. The news channel it was tuned to informed local listeners the eye of the storm was now one hundred miles south of us off the coast of Long Island.

I went to a window and scanned the property and the ocean beyond it. The scene looked apocalyptic. The skies boiled with angry clouds, and the trees were bent practically in half from the strain of the high winds.

It was amazing we hadn't lost power yet, especially as the house was positioned high on the bluffs where the wind tended to be strongest. I went to the thermostat, planning to turn it up a few notches as a preventive measure.

The warmer it was in here, the longer it would take the rooms—especially the upstairs rooms—to get cold in the event of an outage.

But I stopped myself, one hand hovering over the device. If the power went out and the upstairs got cold, Cinda wouldn't be likely to stay up there. She'd be forced to come down here and warm herself by the fire. Which I was about to build.

Smiling, I went into the living room and retrieved the box of matches I'd set out on a side table along with a collection of candles. I lit the kindling under a stack of dried wood in the fireplace.

It smoked and sparked to life, the bright orange flames illuminating the hearth as they ate up the wood shavings.

As the logs themselves caught fire, a pleasant smoky, cedary fragrance filled the room. Soon it would filter upstairs to the room where Cinda hid. Maybe that alone would lure her down here.

Nah—she was so stubborn it would take the discomfort of the cold to drive her down those stairs.

Maybe I should turn the thermostat *down* a few notches?

I resisted the temptation and turned on the TV instead, surfing until I found a movie that looked interesting. Then I put my feet up on the ottoman and settled back into one of the plush sofas to wait her out.

Sometime later I woke with a start. The room was dark. I must have dozed off while watching the movie.

The television was dark as well. There was no sound apart from the faint crackling of the fire and the wind outside. Glancing over toward the kitchen, I searched for the electronic time readout on the stove but couldn't locate it. That confirmed it—the power had gone out.

I got up and added another log to the fire, poking until it flared to new life.

Thankfully there was a stack of wood in a large bin on the porch. We'd need it as the temperature continued to drop. It was already growing cool on the first floor in the areas outside the living room.

Walking to the foot of the stairs, I looked up, listening for any stirring from Cinda's room. Nothing. Either she'd slept through the outage or she was still unwilling to come downstairs.

I went up to my room, took a pillow and the comforter from the bed and went back down to the sofa, stretching out to continue my vigil. Again, I must have dozed because I woke at the sound of a stair creaking.

Keeping my eyes slitted, I watched Cinda tiptoe into the living room, carrying her own pillow and blanket.

I had no idea what time it was—it was still pitch dark out—but I suddenly felt more awake than I ever had in my life.

My pulse pounded, its sound filling my eardrums. I wasn't sure what to do. Should I speak to her, let her know I was awake? That might send her running back up the stairs.

No, I'd stay quiet for now, feign sleep, and let her get settled on the other sofa.

But instead of going to her makeshift bed, Cinda came right to the side of the sofa where I was "sleeping" and stood there looking down at me.

Now my pulse went wild, my heart hammering so hard I was afraid she'd actually hear it from where she stood.

Her knees were at my eye level, and the sweet scent of her perfume or body lotion or whatever it was that made her smell so amazing drifted to my nostrils. I inhaled and let it fill me but kept my eyelids firmly shut, about to die from curiosity.

What was she doing?

Cinda moved, lowering slowly to her knees beside me. She

studied my face, probably searching for signs of wakefulness. I fought to stay still, to keep my breathing quiet and even.

And then she did the most shocking thing.

Leaning forward, she held her face inches from mine for what seemed like hours... then placed the softest kiss on my lips.

Quickly getting to her feet, she hurried over to the other sofa, lay down on it, and covered herself with a blanket.

Meanwhile, I was grateful to be horizontal myself. Otherwise I would have fallen over.

Why had she kissed me? What could it mean?

Cinda had been consistently standoffish to me—when she wasn't being downright hostile.

My mind raced, giving my heart some competition. Both of them charged toward the same conclusion—she still cared for me—or at least felt some residual attraction.

She just didn't want me to know it.

I couldn't stand it any longer. I had to say something.

"I missed you, you know."

It was the absolute truth. It also made me sound pathetic. Her unexpected kiss had clearly knocked something loose in my head.

But now that I'd said it, I wasn't sorry. It *was* true, and whatever had happened to make her stand me up five years ago, I thought she should know the truth.

Cinda didn't move. She didn't even seem to be breathing.

Finally, I heard her voice, soft and quiet in the firelit room.

"I thought you were asleep."

FIFTEEN
You Didn't Know

Cinda

Why why *why* did I do that?

It was stupid, and I knew it. But he'd looked so beautiful, his sleeping face relaxed and peaceful and touched by the glow of firelight.

It had reminded me so much of all the nights we'd sat together on the beach in front of a bonfire, talking for hours and hours.

When Alex had spoken and I'd realized he was awake when I kissed him, I'd almost gotten up and gone back upstairs without a word.

But it was cold up there and *soooo* warm and cozy in here. And I was tired. Tired of trying to dodge him, tired of running from the past.

Tired of wondering and never knowing.

"I was sleeping." The low, graveled sound of Alex's voice backed up his words. "But something woke me."

Right. A kiss. A stupid, idiotic, impulsive kiss. Did he remember it? Maybe he wasn't sure what had awakened him.

He pushed up to one elbow. His hair was rumpled,

somehow making him even more appealing. His eyes roamed over me, taking in my face and bundled-up body.

"Are you cold?"

"Not anymore," I said honestly. My body temperature had skyrocketed in the past minute. "How long has the power been out?"

"I'm not sure. No clock." Alex paused. "Did you hear what I said?"

I wasn't sure how to respond. Of course I'd heard. How could I have missed it?

I missed you, you know.

The words had struck me like a dagger. A rusty one with jagged edges. If he'd missed me so much, why had he never even bothered to contact me after he left?

Talking about it could get complicated. But I wanted to know.

And I supposed the conversation was inevitable. Alex had proved he wasn't going to easily take "no comment" for a response.

I decided to answer his question with one of my own. "Why did you leave?"

"The country? I left because I had to go home with my family. We were going back to Aubernesse. I told you I had to go."

"I know but... well, I thought maybe you'd stay after what happened. At least for a little while."

"What do you mean 'what happened?' After you decided not to meet me on the dock, you mean?" His tone was bewildered. "I thought something horrible had happened to you, you know. I checked all the area hospitals, the police. Then I tried tracking you down, but I finally took the hint. You didn't want to speak to me."

Now I pushed up to my elbow, staring at Alex across the dimly-lit room.

"What are you talking about? My father died. *Of course* I wanted to speak to you."

There was a moment of utter silence.

"Your father died?" he said.

Silence reigned for a few more moments as something became clear to me, something I'd literally never considered as a possibility.

"You didn't know."

It was a statement, not a question. And if Alex didn't know about my father's sudden death, then he never knew why I didn't show up that night for our date.

"No, Cinda. I had no idea. I'm so sorry. When did it happen?"

"That night—at the end of the workday. He had a massive heart attack. I called the ambulance and rode in the back with him. I was at the hospital with him all night while they were trying to save his life. He didn't make it."

"Why didn't you contact me?" he asked. "I would have come. I would have been there with you."

"You didn't have a phone, remember? I asked my stepsister Traci to get a message to you at the club. And I went back there after... you know, the funeral."

Even now a lump stuck in my throat as I recounted the events of those horrible first few days.

"I was told your family had left—gone for the season. I didn't know the name of your hometown or even your real last name. There was no way I could reach you."

Alex's head dropped until he stared at the cushion beneath him. "I can't believe this. All these years I thought you didn't come that night because you didn't want to see me, because you wanted a clean break or something. Do you know I called every "Brown" in the directory looking for you?"

I shook my head, stunned. It had never occurred to me that Alex had tried to reach me and been unable to.

"Why didn't you just call the cleaning company I worked for? The club could have given you the number."

"I did," he said, growing more animated. "That was the *first* place I tried reaching you. The woman who answered the phone said you didn't work there anymore, and she had no idea how to find you—that you were just seasonal help."

My thoughts tangled, trying to make sense of it. "That's crazy. My father owned the company. Everyone who worked there knew me."

I thought for a minute. Who would have answered the phone and told Alex a lie like that?

Julia.

"You must have spoken to my stepmother. I'm not sure why she would have said that, though. She didn't even know about you. She and I weren't exactly close—still aren't."

He shook his head, letting out a loud exhale. "I didn't stop trying until I'd spoken to someone at every Brown household in the state. Maybe I even spoke with your stepmother again at your home. Are you sure she didn't know about me?"

"Alex, *I* didn't even know about you—about your real identity I mean. How could she have?"

"Maybe she routinely lied to young men who called your house asking for you," he suggested. "Or maybe..."

The words died on his lips.

"Alex? What? Maybe what?"

His expression was grave. Actually, no—that was the wrong word. He looked furious.

"Maybe *my* parents knew about *you*. When I get back to the mainland, I'll be having a *serious* conversation with them."

"You think they did something to interfere? To keep you from finding me?"

"I wouldn't put it past them. My father is a means-justify-the-ends kind of person. And he places duty above all else. Maybe he found out about the ring."

My heart seized, flashing from hot to cold to hot again. Suddenly sweltering, I threw off my covers and sat upright.

"What ring?"

Alex took a deep breath and met my eyes directly before answering. "I asked you to meet me that night because... there was something I wanted to ask you. Something life-changing."

I felt light-headed. My heartbeat roared in my ears, threatening to drown out Alex's next words.

"I wanted to meet at the docks because I'd hired a boat to bring us here—to this house," he said. "A house I'd bought for us. Me and you. I knew my parents wouldn't approve, that they'd do everything possible to change my mind. They had something else planned for my life—a political marriage that would benefit our country. That's why I didn't tell them. But maybe someone did."

"Alex," I whispered. I honestly didn't know what else to say. And I had no breath to say it with anyway.

"I'm so sorry I wasn't there for you, Cinda. I'm sorry I gave up on us. I should have known." He swallowed. "I loved you. I was planning to give up the throne, my home—even my family for you if necessary. I would never have left you to go through that alone if I'd known."

If, if, and if. What a hateful word. If only I'd known the real reason I'd never heard from Alex again.

If only so much time hadn't passed. If only life hadn't moved on since then.

If only I didn't have so much to lose.

"I'm sorry, too," I said, fighting back tears. "I'm sorry you believed I stood you up. I hate to think of you standing all alone out there on that dock."

That was when I lost the battle. A choked sob clogged my throat, preventing any further words. I brought my hands up to cover my face, embarrassed to break down like this in front of him.

Within moments, Alex was there, kneeling in front of me. His arms went around me, pulling my wet face against his neck, a large hand running up and down my back in soothing strokes.

It was the first time we'd touched in years, and the contact was heavenly.

"Don't cry," he said and made a *shhhh* noise as he continued to rub my back. "Don't cry. It's okay. It wasn't your fault. At least now we know the truth."

He shifted back so he could see my face. His was far too close, and the look in his eyes was far too tender.

His hands on my shoulders were too gentle. For a moment I thought he might kiss me.

And that I might want him to.

Alex's voice was filled with emotion when he spoke again. "There's so much I want to know about you—what your life is like now, what happened with you the past five years."

In an instant my insides chilled, reality intruding on the magical moment like an icy breeze through a door blown open during a blizzard.

Our mutual revelations about the end of our relationship didn't change anything.

It *had* ended. And the risk of my losing AJ was still just as great.

I didn't know how Alex had changed over the past five years either—or how he might react to finding out he had a son.

My phone rang. *Saved by the bell—literally.*

I scrambled for it, profoundly grateful for the excuse to remove myself from Alex's too-tempting proximity.

"I have to take this. Excuse me."

SIXTEEN
Irate Caveman

Alex

Cinda gripped the phone like it was a lifeline.

Walking quickly away toward the cold, dark dining room, she answered. "Hello?" A pause as she listened. "Oh, hi sweetie."

Sweetie? She closed the dining room door behind her, so I couldn't hear the next few words. But I desperately wanted to.

Feeling like a total creeper, I got up and tiptoed toward the dining room, pressing my ear against the door.

Cinda's voice on the other side sounded like marshmallows dipped in honey, soft and sweet.

"What are you doing up so late? Oh, you couldn't sleep? Is the storm keeping you awake?"

With every soothing word, the rock in my stomach gained weight. She assured the person on the other end of the line she'd be home soon and that she missed him, and jealousy blazed in my gut like a fresh twig thrown into a roaring fire.

Which was absurd. We hadn't seen each other in years. I had zero right to be jealous. I'd dated other people since then too.

But unlike me, Cinda *had* apparently fallen in love with someone new.

I couldn't keep myself from wishing it was me that she spoke to with such obvious affection, me that she was promising to get home to as soon as possible.

Just before hanging up, she drove the final nail into the coffin of my newly formed hopes. She told the guy, "I love you."

The dining room door opened suddenly, and I stumbled backward. *So busted.*

Clearly surprised to find me standing on the other side, Cinda jumped. "What are you doing?"

Thinking fast, I offered my arm. "Making sure you don't trip in the dark."

She narrowed her eyes at me but allowed me to lead her back into the warmth and light of the living room. Trying desperately to keep my voice casual, I asked, "Who was that?"

My attempt at nonchalance must have failed because her expression changed. For some reason she looked... *resigned*, for lack of a better word.

"You were listening?" she asked.

"You're in love with him," I stated the obvious.

Cinda bit her lip, her eyebrows drawn together in a pensive expression. "I wouldn't say 'in love.'"

"But you do love him."

"Yes. I do... but that was not what you think it was."

Right. I wasn't stupid—I knew what I'd heard. There had been love in her voice.

"Tell me that wasn't a guy," I challenged, pointing at the phone still in her hand.

Cinda hesitated, her eyes searching the room before coming back to meet mine. "I can't."

"So, you have a serious boyfriend. You love him. Why don't you want to talk about it?"

And why was I acting like this? I had no right to ask. It was none of my business. But I couldn't seem to stop. I had to know. Hearing Cinda speaking those sweet words to another guy had apparently driven me beyond the point of reason.

She looked like she was on the verge of crying. Which made no sense. "I don't have a boyfriend, okay? I don't date."

Wait… *what?*

"Look, a lot has changed since we were together," she said. "I'm a totally different person now. So are you. There's no need for us to bare our souls at this point."

Cinda pulled away from my grip, grabbing her pillow from the sofa before rushing toward the stairs. "I'm going to sleep in my room."

I was right on her heels. "Oh no you don't. You're not running away this time. Why don't you date? *Cinda.* Why did you say you have no plans to marry? Answer me."

Picking up speed, she reached the dark staircase and started running up, taking the stairs two at a time.

"Cinda," I repeated, still following and growing hotter by the second. "Did something happen to you? I can find out, you know. I have billions of dollars at my disposal, so you might as well tell me."

"Leave me alone," she yelled back over her shoulder.

My exasperation converted to fear in an instant when she lost her footing. With a yelp, she went down, falling hard on the wooden stairs.

Instinctively, I reached out, stopping her from rolling any farther down the staircase. Lowering myself, I sat on a riser beside her, my arm going around her back to steady her.

"Are you okay?"

Her head shook in tiny jerks. Though she didn't cry out, she was rocking back and forth, holding her ankle and whimpering in pain.

"I think it might be broken."

Oh no. Please don't let it be broken.

Block Island had a medical center, but it would be closed at this hour even if there was no storm raging outside.

It was too dark on the stairs to check her injury, so I scooped Cinda up and carried her back down to the sofa. Kneeling beside it, I propped the ankle she was favoring on a cushion.

"Let me look at it," I said in a tone that left no room for argument.

She nodded her consent, now squeezing her eyes tightly closed. Lying back on her pillow, she breathed rapidly through her nose as I turned her leg and gingerly prodded the ankle with my fingertips.

"I don't think it's broken," I said, breathing a sigh of relief. "I'm no expert, but I've twisted my ankle a few times playing sports. I think you might have stretched or torn some ligaments."

I turned to check her face, feeling more than a little guilty. It was hard to be sure with the low lighting, but she looked pale to me.

"How much pain are you in?"

She panted. "It's okay. Not so bad." But a thin sheen of sweat had broken out on her upper lip, and she was grimacing.

"Liar." I rose to my feet. "There are some first aid supplies and pain reliever up in my bathroom. Be right back."

Grabbing a candle to light my way, I went upstairs, found the kit, and rushed back down.

"I found some ice packs."

Taking one out of its wrapper, I squeezed and shook it and laid it on her ankle. Then I cut a strip of gauze and wrapped it around her foot to hold the ice pack in place.

"Okay, now for the pain." I shook three tablets into my

hand and went to get a glass of water from the kitchen, offering them to her. "Take these. They'll help."

She nodded, reached for the pills and the glass. "What are they?"

"The two red ones are ibuprofen. The white one's a muscle relaxer. It'll make you drowsy and hopefully help you sleep."

She swallowed all three. "Thanks."

"What else can I do?"

"Nothing. I'll be okay," she said, then her eyes met mine. "I'm sorry."

Shame twisted my stomach into a tight knot. "Don't apologize. It's not your fault. It was dark, and an irate caveman was chasing you. I should be apologizing to you for being so pushy."

"No, I mean I'm sorry for running away like that. About... not telling you."

My heart stopped for a moment before picking up again in a new, faster rhythm. "Telling me what?"

"Who I was talking to. It was... my son."

All the breath left my lungs in a rush. My head spun as I tried to process the shock. "You have a child?"

In all my daydreams about Cinda over the years, I'd never imagined her with a baby.

"Yes. He's with my friend Kristal tonight. He's afraid of storms and is having a hard time sleeping. He's why I was so determined to get home today."

"So... you're divorced."

Cinda shook her head. "No. I never married."

She kept her gaze trained on her lap. She was quiet, almost as if she was waiting for something. Judgment? Condemnation?

Speculation?

A new feeling invaded my chest, a burning sensation that

was equal parts excitement and outrage as sparks of suspicion landed and ignited inside me.

My tone was low and deliberate when I asked the next logical question.

"Who is his father?"

SEVENTEEN

My First and Only

Cinda

Tremors shook my body. The moment I'd been dreading was here, and I was *so* not ready for it.

Alex was trembling too, and his breathing sounded weird. It was possible *I* might have to administer some first aid because he looked like he was on the verge of passing out.

"His father is..." At the last second I swerved. "...not in the picture."

It was true. I *couldn't* tell him the whole truth. Not while we were trapped here together. Not without knowing how he'd react, what he might do with the information.

"We were together only a short while. And he's... got his own life. He's not the family-man type."

I rushed to add, "It's fine. AJ and I get along just fine. We don't need him."

Studying his face, I waited, struggling to keep my expression neutral and my breathing even.

Had he bought my non-answer? Or did he see through my bluff?

He knew I'd been a virgin when we'd started our relationship. Could he somehow tell there'd been no one after him? That he was my first and only?

The wait was killing me, those penetrating deep brown eyes making me feel like the layers of secrecy I'd worn like armor were being peeled back with painstaking slowness.

Alex's expression changed then, softening until he almost looked like he was in pain. "That can't be easy—being a single mother."

I nearly sagged in relief. *This* I could talk about.

"No. It's not easy," I admitted. "But my baby's worth any sacrifice. That's why I don't date. When you're a single parent and running a business, it doesn't leave much time for a social life."

Alex nodded. "I see."

Was it my imagination, or was there a hint of satisfaction in the smile sneaking across his lips?

"I'd love to see him," he said. "Do you have some pictures with you?"

"Of course. On my—" A swift realization cut off my answer. The instant Alex saw AJ he'd *know*. The boy was practically a clone of my long-lost love.

"Oh… they're on my phone, but the battery died," I lied.

Alex's smile dimmed. "That's too bad. I guess I'll have to wait till we get power back. Can you tell me about him? What's he like?"

He's like you, my mind screamed. *In so many ways.* How was I supposed to do this? Talk about AJ to his father… who didn't know he even had a child.

Panic simmered just beneath my skin. I *couldn't* do this.

Faking a wide yawn, I closed my eyes in a long blink. "I think the muscle relaxer is kicking in," I said, dragging my lids open again with overdone effort.

"Oh. Right. I should... let you get some sleep."

Alex hesitated for another moment, scanning my face and body before rising and going back to his own makeshift bed across the room. "Need anything before I lie down?"

"No. I'm fine. I'll probably go right to sleep. You should too." *Please, please go to sleep.*

I did *not* go right to sleep. It was impossible with Alexander Wessex only a few feet away. And I wasn't fine. Far from it.

My whole being was caught up in a fierce longing I hadn't experienced in... well, in about five years, since I'd last been with Alex.

It was colder without him next to me. Though I knew it was foolish, I kind of regretted sending him to the other couch instead of asking him to lie down beside me and hold me the way I'd dreamed of him doing during the countless lonely nights we'd been apart.

Why did *this* man, above all the others in the world, have the unique ability to affect me like this, to overtake my mind and heart and upset my usual certainty in my own plans for my life?

At some point I must have fallen asleep because I found myself in a nightmare.

It had something to do with the hurricane, but in my dream, it seemed more like a tornado event with terrifying dark funnel clouds all around. I ran around my small house, frantically checking the closets and under the beds, searching for AJ.

He was frightened and alone, and I had to get to him. At one point I spotted Alex and begged him to help me, to find our son, to save him.

"Cinda?"

A gentle shake blurred the frightening images, sending a

ripple of reality through them like a water droplet disturbing a still pool.

"Cinda, you okay? Having a bad dream?"

"Alex?" I opened my eyes, blinking in confusion at the deep male voice and the outline of wide shoulders and messy dark hair shining in the waning firelight.

"Where's AJ?"

"It's okay," he soothed, stroking my tear-dampened hair back from my cheek. "Everything's okay. He's safe with your friend Kristal. You were having a nightmare. Maybe I shouldn't have given you that muscle relaxer. They can cause bad dreams in some people."

Sitting up slightly, I became more alert. "It was just a dream," I said, mostly to myself.

"Just a dream," Alex confirmed. "Want to tell me what it was about?"

I waved a hand in front of my face as if clearing away a wisp of smoke from an extinguished candle flame. "No. It was nothing. I can't even really remember it."

"You were calling my name."

I blinked again, this time from surprise. "I was?"

"Yes, over and over again. You sounded scared. Was something bad happening to you?"

"No, to—" I stopped myself abruptly. I'd almost said, "to our son." Instead, I began again, saying, "It was AJ. He was lost."

"You're worried about him," Alex said. "Even in your sleep. I'm sorry I made you come out here. You should be home with your child."

I shook my head. "It's okay. What you said is true. He *is* safe with Kristal. And when I spoke to him earlier, he sounded happy by the time we hung up. He just misses me. I miss him too. We've hardly been apart since he was born."

"How old is he?" Alex asked, his voice gentle.

He was obviously trying to comfort me, but the question had the opposite effect. My heart rate rocketed.

Every conversation I had with Alex was fraught with danger. One wrong word, and he'd figure out what I was hiding.

"He's little. Just a toddler," I said.

Some people might consider a four-year-old a toddler, right? Although with the way my son ran and jumped and climbed everything in sight, his toddling days were long past.

Alex nodded. "Does he look like you?"

My pulse still racing, I answered honestly. "He looks like his father, actually."

"That's too bad."

He stroked wisps of hair back from my forehead with his fingertips then let the back of one glide over my cheekbone. "I used to think if we ever had children, I'd want them to look exactly like their lovely mother."

Panic lit a signal fire inside my heart, alerting my brain it was time to take evasive action. I knew that look in Alex's eyes. I'd seen it many times before.

He was thinking about kissing me.

It didn't matter how long it had been since I'd kissed a man, or how incredibly handsome Alex looked, or how cozy and romantic the firelit room was—I couldn't go *there.*

Not with him.

Not again.

I struggled to sit up. "I need to..."

What? I grappled for an excuse to burst this bubble of intimacy that seemed to have formed around the two of us in the last minute. It felt too good. It felt like it *used* to feel between us—before Alex had vanished from my life.

I blurted the first thing that came to mind. "I need to pee."

His eyebrows shot up, and the spell was broken. Nothing like mentioning bodily functions to ruin the mood.

"Oh. Of course. Here, let me help you."

"No." Putting a hand on his chest, I rebuffed Alex's attempt to lift me. "I can go by myself."

I could think of few things more humiliating than being carried to the toilet by Prince Alexander Wessex of Aubernesse. And I wasn't used to depending on anyone for anything. Hated it, in fact.

My self-sufficient attitude came to a swift and painful halt when I attempted to stand. And fell back onto the sofa, wincing and clutching my ankle.

"I don't think I can put any weight on it." And now that I was thinking about it, I actually *did* need to pee. *Great.*

As it turned out, he didn't carry me, but he did provide a personal escort, one slow step-hop at a time. When we were inside the bathroom, Alex gave me an uncertain look.

"Do you want me to... stay?"

"No," I yelped. Then more quietly, I said, "No, thank you. I can hold on to the wall and the vanity counter. I'll be fine."

"Okay. Well, I'll go to the kitchen and get a glass of water for you. It's time for another dose of pain medication. I think we'll skip the muscle relaxer this time."

"Okay. That's probably a good idea because I still feel a little loopy."

He gave me another long look as if unsure he should leave me.

"Not *that* loopy. I'm not going to fall in," I told him.

"Right. All right then. Be back in a few minutes."

When I was safely settled onto the couch again, Alex handed me the water glass and two more ibuprofen tablets. He watched as I swallowed them then restacked the pillows at the foot of the couch and helped me lift my leg to prop my throbbing ankle.

"I need to change your ice packs. They're not cold enough anymore."

"Don't worry about it. I'm sure it'll be fine by morning."

"Not if we don't keep it iced." Alex reached into the first aid kit and grabbed two new cold packs, squeezing and shaking to activate them. "Okay, hold still. I've got to unwrap the gauze."

He used excessive care unwrapping my swollen ankle, which had now turned all sorts of lovely colors, removing the old cold packs and replacing them. Throughout it all, he kept sneaking glances at my face, checking for pain reaction, I assumed. It was touching, actually.

"It's weird to have someone take care of me," I said softly. "Usually I'm the one doing the caretaking."

"*That*—is a true shame. And it's truly my pleasure."

Alex stared at me for a long moment, his eyes squinting in concentration. "Why *are* you alone? I know what you said about not having time because you're a single mum... but single parents *do* date. And you're far too young to have given up on the whole enterprise. So it's a choice—it must be because there's no way you haven't had plenty of opportunity. Either that or there's something seriously wrong with American men."

"Well, that's up for debate" I laughed. "Just kidding. But you're right. It is a choice. I just... I don't want to make a mistake. Because of AJ. I can't bring just anyone into his life, you know? He's so little, so helpless. His heart is so sweet and pure. I can't even think about someone hurting him in any way. I have to be careful."

"I understand." He shook his head. "I still can't believe you're a mother. Don't get me wrong, I can totally see it—how you'd be an amazing, loving mum. I can tell that you are. But well, I guess my mind just refuses to picture you with another man... no matter how short the relationship might have been."

Desperate to change the topic, I said, "I'm sure your love

life is a much more interesting subject. I'll bet *you* haven't been lonely all these years."

Alex chuckled, but then his expression turned serious. "You know what? I was. I mean, yes, I've dated from time to time, but there's been no one special."

Another long pause. "And I thought perhaps... well, I wondered... I wondered if you'd chosen to remain alone because of what happened between us. Because you... you gave me your virginity, and then I vanished. I thought it might have left you... well, *reluctant* to get into new relationships. I'm sorry for that—sorrier than you can even imagine. I would never have hurt you willingly."

For a moment I couldn't draw air because Alex's words seemed to have siphoned the entire oxygen supply from the room. Not only were they unexpected, but he'd seen through my bluff about being "too busy" to date and read my heart with laser-like precision.

"I believe you," I finally said. "Thank you for saying that." Taking a fortifying breath, I continued. "And you're right. I have been squeamish about romantic entanglements."

"Except for AJ's father," he prompted.

"Yes," I rushed to agree. "That's right. Except for him."

"I can't help but surmise he was a disappointment as well," Alex said. "Whatever the reason that one didn't work out, well, I just want you to know you deserve better than to be left to raise a child alone. You deserve to have everything you want. When we met nearly five years ago, I thought you were the most beautiful, cleverest, most amazing woman I'd ever met. Now... well, you simply astonish me."

His eyes dropped to my lips, and I realized he'd been leaning closer and closer as we talked.

"What are you doing?" I whispered. He didn't answer, just kept angling toward me until his face was just above mine, and his mouth was only inches away.

"Cinda?" he whispered.

My heart fluttered like the wings of the hummingbirds AJ loved to watch at the feeder outside our kitchen window.

"Yes?"

Alex's large body shifted toward me, depressing the sofa cushion, causing me to roll toward him, and—

"Ow!" I yelped as pain radiated from my ankle up my leg. Mesmerized by the intention in his eyes, I'd forgotten all about my sprain. Now I had no choice but to remember it.

"Ow ow ow." Pain sang through my leg like an opera diva powering through the final notes of a performance.

"Oh, your ankle." Alex stood and moved back away from the sofa. "I'm so sorry. I don't know what I was thinking. I just wanted... never mind. Forgive me. How much does it hurt?"

I grimaced. "It's not bad."

"That's not true. I hurt you. I feel terrible. How stupid of me. Can I get you something? More pain reliever? A new ice pack?"

I smiled at him. "No, I'm okay. I promise. It's better now."

"Okay good."

Shaking out his arms and hands, Alex backed away but kept eye contact with me. He hooked a thumb over one shoulder.

"So... I think I'd better go back to my own sofa—and stay there." He gave a nervous sounding laugh.

I nodded. I knew exactly how he felt. If I'd been ambulatory, I'd be backing away myself. Being close to him was too tempting. Tempting and scary and wonderful.

And scary.

Had he been about to kiss me? Or had I only been wishing he would?

Ooh. Bad. Bad, Cinda. No kissing.

And *definitely* no wishing. Either of those things would only confuse this already confusing situation even further.

"That's probably a good idea," I said. "And we really should try to get some sleep before the sun comes up."

"Yes. You're right." Still watching me, Alex slid under the blanket on the other couch. "Goodnight Cinda."

"Goodnight Alex. Sleep well."

EIGHTEEN

Mermaid Retrieval

Cinda

I wasn't sure what time Alex got up or if he'd managed to sleep well, but when I woke in the morning, he was in the kitchen.

Cooking. Apparently, the gas stove still functioned with the electricity out. Whatever he was making smelled good.

Sitting up on the couch, I looked around and blinked in the hazy daylight like a kitten with newly opened eyes.

"Good morning," Alex said in a cheery tone, turning to transfer the fragrant food from a skillet onto a plate waiting on the counter. "How's your ankle feeling today?"

I looked at the ankle in question, wincing as I moved it gingerly. "Better, I think? A bit tender. It's swollen, though. And colorful."

Pinks and purples and even a bit of black covered the skin, and my ankle looked at least twice its normal circumference.

"I saw that. Even with proper treatment that would have been inevitable. And with only 'Dr. Wessex's' questionable skills at your service... I'm afraid you may be in for a bit of a protracted recovery period."

Alex came into the living room carrying the plate which he set on the low table in front of the sofa. He offered me a steaming mug. "The coffeemaker's electric, but I found some tea bags and a kettle. Do you still like tea?"

"Yes."

"There's sugar if you'd like it. No cream obviously."

I lifted the cup and took an exploratory sip. "Sugar would be great, thank you. How long have you been up?"

Alex walked back to the kitchen to fetch the sugar bowl. "A while," he answered with a smile. "I'm still on Aubernesse time, and my sleep schedule is all out of whack. I'm glad you managed to sleep. I was worried the pain might keep you awake."

"I woke a few times, but I managed to get through the night."

What I didn't say was that each time I'd awakened, I'd immediately checked the sofa opposite mine, searching for the reassuring shape of Alex's large body stretched out nearby.

And it *had* given me comfort to see him there. Which made no sense at all.

"Have you heard any weather updates today?"

Alex returned and sat on the floor beside my sofa, taking my cup and stirring sugar into it before returning it to my hands.

"I have. I monitored the reports throughout the night in case I needed to snatch you up and heroically carry you to the basement." He gave me a playful smirk. "They've downgraded the system to a tropical storm, though it's a nasty one. It's strong, but I don't think we need to fear blowing away. Power's still out obviously."

"So... no ferry service today?"

He chuckled at my hopeful tone. "No ferry service. No flying either. Too risky. They're saying the worst of it will pass by tonight. We should be able to get you home by noon tomorrow. As for today… I'm afraid you're stuck here with me."

I'm afraid, too. What were we going to *do* all day, just the two of us alone in this big old house?

I quashed a flurry of inappropriate thoughts and an uprising of butterfly wings in my belly, faking nonchalance with a shrug. "Well, what can you do?"

Alex rose and looked down at me. "I, for one, intend to take a long, hot shower. That sofa was not exactly a great mattress."

"Is there hot water?"

"We've got a gas-powered hot water heater here. Besides, hot water will last in the tank for several days in an outage."

I gave my sprained ankle a morose look. "Sounds good. I'm jealous."

"I'll be happy to pick you up and bring you along. We could share the shower, conserve that hot water—just in case." He shot me the same wicked grin that had turned me inside out as a young twenty-something.

"You wish," I quipped back.

Alex stopped and pinned me with that arresting gaze of his. "Indeed, I do."

Memories of past intimacies flooded my brain, shooting darts of heat to my breasts and lower abdomen, making me squirm.

I grabbed a decorative pillow from the floor next to the sofa and tossed it at his head. "Go. And take your flirty-dirty Euro sense of humor with you. It needs to be washed out with soap."

He ducked and laughed, heading for the stairs. "Need anything before I go? An escort to the loo perhaps?"

"I'm fine for now. Just go."

Alex had reached the top of the staircase before my cheeks finally cooled and my lady parts agreed to stand down. He'd always known exactly how to fluster me—and he was even better at it now.

While a shared shower was out of the question, I *was* desperate to bathe. Especially after Alex returned twenty minutes later, looking—and smelling—clean and fresh. I hated feeling sweaty and dirty while he looked and smelled so utterly amazing. It wasn't fair.

But I couldn't stand in the shower. Even a bath was impossible. How would I get into the tub with my bum ankle? There was no way I could do it on my own.

There was also no way I'd ask Alex for help. How would that even work? He'd have to lift my naked body and lower me into the water.

The aforementioned lady bits woke right back up and did a round of morning affirmations.

We are beautiful.

We are worthy of attention.

We've been neglected for far too long and

We are beyond *ready for a little fun.*

Ugh. No. There would be no bath. And *definitely* no fun.

As if reading my mind, Alex asked, "Want me to draw a bath for you in the first-floor guest bathroom? It looks like Janey left some bubble stuff in there."

I pouted. "I can't. My ankle."

"It's fine to get it wet—oh..."

A look of understanding crossed his face. He appeared to ponder it a moment.

"What if I were to carry you in there, set you down on the bathmat beside the tub and leave while you undress?" he suggested. "There are plenty of clean towels. You could wrap yourself in one, then I could come in and put you in the water. When you're done, just wrap it around yourself again and call for me. I'll lift you out and set you down again so you can dry off and dress."

"I guess that could work." My hopes began to rise but then sank again. "I don't know if I'm comfortable with you seeing me with just a towel on though."

Or holding me with just a towel on. Or touching my bare skin—anywhere at all.

Alex laughed. "Cinda—it's not like we're strangers. I saw you every day of the summer in just a swimsuit." His brow went up. "And on a couple of occasions in even less."

I held up my hand to stop him. "Okay, okay fine. You're right."

"Good." He knelt to lift me. "Put your arms around my neck then."

When I complied, Alex swept me up and carried me to the bathroom.

"I've gained a little weight since you last saw me," I said, suddenly self-conscious. "Having a baby will do that to you."

"Please. You look fantastic. Even better than before."

Embarrassed—and yes, a little pleased—I pushed my heated cheek against Alex's shoulder. "Liar."

"I'm completely serious. You looked like a girl back then. Now you're a gorgeous woman. I'd go on but as your cheeks are already red as apples, I'll leave it at that."

"Thank you."

Alex stoppered the bathtub and started the water to fill it before leaving to give me privacy. I undressed awkwardly then wrapped a bath sheet around myself.

"Okay, you can come in now."

He must have been waiting just outside the door because he immediately entered. His lips quirked to the side in a grin he tried, but failed, to hide.

"You look a bit like a stranded mermaid down there."

I pointed a warning finger in his direction. "Don't laugh at me. I feel silly enough already."

"I've always wanted to rescue a mermaid." He bent over and scooped me up. "It *is* a job for a prince after all."

"You've got the wrong story, Prince Charming. And the wrong girl."

"We'll see about that. Let's get you in the water and find out if you grow fins."

Lifting me easily, Alex lowered my towel-clad body gently into the hot bathwater, soaking his arms to the elbows.

He stood and looked down at me a moment. "You okay? Feel all right? Not dizzy or anything?" Glancing over at the doorway, he furrowed his brow. "Maybe I should sit just outside there with the door open in case you need me."

I raised a wet hand and moved it in a dismissive gesture, flicking water droplets onto the floor surrounding the tub.

"No. I'm fine. I'll be in here a while."

And there's no way I can relax with you sitting there listening to every splash and movement.

"Why don't you go read a book or something? You've spent far too much time taking care of me."

"Not enough time in my view." Alex walked quickly to the door and turned back to add, "Call me when you're ready to get out."

Pulling the door closed, he left.

Not enough time? What had he meant by that?

Was he trying to say he *wanted* to take care of me?

Well, I didn't need anyone to take care of me—not usually anyway. These were extreme circumstances.

And you could do a whole hell of a lot worse than having Alexander Wessex as your nurse and lady's maid.

I laughed lightly and sank deeper into the steamy bath, enjoying the feel of the warm heat on my skin and muscles, relaxing fully now that Alex had left the room.

When the water had begun to turn tepid and my fingers had pruned, I wrapped the heavy, soaked towel around my body again, tucking the top edge tightly under one arm and pulling the lower edge down to cover my thighs. I'd actually have to hold that in place because the water kept floating it up.

With my good foot I kicked the lever to release the drain mechanism then called for Alex. He opened the door so quickly I suspected he may have been waiting outside it after all.

"Have a nice bath?" he asked as he approached the tub.

I didn't answer right away. I couldn't. Alex was shirtless.

His feet were bare, and he wore only a pair of black running shorts.

As he'd mentioned earlier, we'd seen each other in bathing suits nearly every day of that long-ago summer. But it *had* been long ago. I'd been in the company of very few shirtless men since then, and *none* of them had looked like this.

Even Alex hadn't looked like this back then.

He'd always had an attractive physique, tall and broad-shouldered with great muscle tone. But he'd been thinner then, lanky as young men often are.

Now, at age thirty, he was a male in his prime. His arms and chest were filled out with firm muscle, as were his legs.

Like the majority of people native to his European home country, his skin was olive-toned. His was taut and sun-bronzed and made my fingers itch to reach out and stroke it.

His stomach was... oh good God I was staring. I needed to look away from all that tan skin and segmented muscle, or I wasn't going to be able to handle it when he—

Too late. Alex lifted me and held my dripping wet body against him, and now my warm skin was pressed against his, and that amazing scent I'd detected earlier was right there, and, and...

Mind on the game. Off *the hot man. On. The. Game.*

Say something. Make conversation.

"Were you... exercising?"

He barked a short laugh. "No. Why do you ask? Do I smell like a locker room or something?"

"No. You... took off your clothes."

He grinned widely. "This is my mermaid-retrieval uniform."

When I gave him a dazed look, he explained in a tone of voice one would use with a small child. "I don't have that many changes of clothes here, and we can't exactly hang things outside to dry. I knew I was bound to get soaked while fishing you out of the tub."

I craned my neck to see water running down Alex's long legs and pooling on the bathroom floor around his feet. "Oh. Right. Sorry about that."

"No worries. I just wanted to be prepared." He set me on the bathroom rug and gestured toward the shorts. "These will dry off pretty quickly in front of the fire. When you're dressed, I'll take you there too, so your hair can dry and you don't catch a chill."

He held up a finger. "Which reminds me..."

Alex left the bathroom and came back a moment later with a large man's bathrobe. "I couldn't find anything left in Janey's room, but I did find this hanging in the master closet. Must be Cameron's. It seemed like a better option than the pajamas you had on or your clothes from yesterday. The house is a bit chilly."

I took it from him gratefully. "Yes. Thank you. It's perfect."

Anything to get you and your sexy, shirtless self out of my line of sight as soon as possible.

NINETEEN
Genetic Gifts

Cinda

Once I had the robe on, I wasn't so sure.

It was long and covered everything decently, especially as I had the belt cinched around my waist as securely as possible. But I'd have to be careful with the split in the front. In any case, I was eager to get in front of that roaring fire Alex had mentioned.

I called him, and he carried me into the living room, depositing me on the soft rug in front of the fireplace. True to his word, he'd built the fire up until it blazed strongly and threw all the toasty heat I could have hoped for.

I stretched out my toes toward the hearth and gazed into it as I brushed my wet hair, hoping the brushing would help it dry faster.

"You look the way you did when you used to come in from the beach."

Chill bumps spread over my skin—more an effect, I suspected, of Alex's smooth, cultured voice behind me than the pleasant heat surrounding me.

I glanced back over one shoulder at him. "Waterlogged and frizzy-headed?"

He gave me a slow, appreciative smile. "No. Fresh-faced and natural." He let a beat pass. "And breathtakingly beautiful."

"Alex," I pleaded. "Don't."

I couldn't stand the way his words made my heart thump. His sweet, nostalgic tone and heated gazes were even worse.

"Don't what? Tell you you're beautiful? Okay, fine. What shall we talk about then?"

He came and sat on the edge of the wide stone hearth, far too close for comfort. "We've got all day. Why don't you fill me in on the past five years of your life? I'd love to hear it. Every last detail."

The thumping shifted into a frantic scattering of beats. That would be even worse. My mind scrambled, searching for an escape. "Do you have any games here?"

"Games?" Alex's momentary puzzlement melted into a knowing grin. "How about truth or dare?"

"No," I yelped. "I mean, I was thinking more along the lines of Scrabble or Monopoly." Yes, that would be a good one—it took forever to play. "Or maybe cards or dice?"

His playful expression dissipated, replaced by a hard scrutiny. He could tell I was trying to avoid real conversation.

"A game would really take my mind off my ankle."

Properly guilt-tripped now, Alex rose from his spot on the hearth and began checking the cabinet beneath the large television and the ones on either side.

"I know I didn't leave any here," he said. "But maybe Cam or Janey did."

After a thorough search during which he found no games—not even a single die—he turned to me and gave me the upturned empty hands gesture. "I'm afraid there's nothing."

"What about the kitchen cabinets?" I suggested, growing desperate.

Alex dutifully trodded to the kitchen and performed a search of the cabinets there as well. After a minute, he said, "I found something."

I turned my head to see him holding up a dark glass bottle.

"For spin the bottle?" he teased.

Instantly, my heart kicked into high gear. Images swarmed my mind—kisses Alex and I had shared in the past—a mental movie of our bodies entwined, groaning and devouring each other until we were both exhausted and satisfied.

Those collided with fresher images of the look in Alex's eyes last night as he'd moved closer and closer to me on the sofa, the way he'd leaned in with his gaze trained on my lips.

"No thank you," I said in a prim tone manufactured to cover my breathlessness. "Maybe we could listen to music. Oh, wait... I guess we need to save the radio battery for checking weather updates."

Alex strode back into the living room. "I have an idea."

Going to the clear Lucite bench in front of the fantastic transparent baby grand, he sat—still shirtless mind you—and placed his fingers on the keys.

He tossed me a cocky grin. "The lady wants music... she shall have it."

And then he started playing. If I hadn't been on the floor already, I might have swooned and ended up there, watching and listening to Alex play.

His fingers moved over the keys like flowing water, or perhaps a magic wand casting a spell. The sounds he drew from the piano were stunningly beautiful, barely resembling the comparatively clunky notes my own hand-me-down instrument produced.

I'd bought it dirt cheap at an estate sale so AJ could learn to play. My four-year-old had taken to it immediately, surpassing my own meager skills within weeks of beginning lessons.

Tears filled my eyes as I continued to listen to Alex's skillful, emotional playing, and my heart ache increased with each chord progression. When he finished the song, he looked up, meeting my eyes. His were tight, almost as if he was worried about my opinion.

"It was beautiful," I told him honestly. "Absolutely exquisite. What was the song? What's it called?"

Alex's shoulders lifted and fell in a slight shrug. His tone was dismissive. "Just something I wrote."

I nodded, not surprised. "I didn't know you played piano. I remember you playing guitar, of course."

How could I forget? He'd been smiling at me and making flirty remarks for days, asking me out repeatedly. Naturally, I'd been tempted, but fraternizing with the beach club members was strictly prohibited. So I'd declined his offers, remaining polite and professional.

Until one night after dusk when some of the club's younger members had gathered around a bonfire in the sand. Alex had brought out a guitar. I'd been a goner.

Having finished my work for the day, I had found a spot in the shadows outside the light of the fire, watching and listening as he entertained the group with a selection of James Taylor and Beatles songs, each one more beautiful than the last.

I thought he hadn't even realized I was there, but when he took a break, Alex walked directly to me, sank into the sand beside me, and gave me a dazzling grin.

"Any requests?" he'd asked.

How am I supposed to keep resisting this guy?

That was the impossible question. Then and now.

"I *didn't* play piano back then," Alex said, bringing me

out of my reverie. "I remember you said you did. I decided to learn."

"Yes, well, I *never* played like you do, even after years of lessons."

"Are you giving AJ lessons?"

I laughed. "More like he's teaching *me*. He's amazing. It's almost as if he was born to play."

Alex smiled. "Maybe he was. Some people just have an innate gift for music. My mum says I was always drawn to it, from the earliest age. Like her."

My heart froze. This conversation was headed in a dangerous direction. We should *not* be discussing hereditary musical talent or any other sort of genetic gifts.

I forced a smile. "Will you play something else?"

He set his hands on the keys again, and this time I recognized the tune instantly. It was "The Long and Winding Road" by the Beatles. My favorite.

Had he remembered that, or was it coincidental? Either way, the ballad about fated lovers who always found their way back to one another (at least the way I'd always interpreted it) turned on the waterworks.

As Alex finished playing, he looked up and saw my tears. "Do you remember me playing this for you?"

I nodded and swiped beneath my eyes. "I remember."

"Shall I play another?"

"I'm not sure I can take another." I sniffled as I laughed. "Would you mind getting me a tissue?"

He was on his feet and heading to fulfill my request as soon as it left my lips. "Of course. I'll be right back. Need anything else?"

I hesitated a beat and then surrendered. It was no use. I couldn't fight it any longer.

I gave in to the longing, deciding to satisfy my hunger to learn about his life in the years we'd been apart. This unexpected interlude would be all we'd ever have—all we *could* have—but I would take advantage of it and do my best to reclaim every minute of the time we'd lost.

"Yes," I called to him. "That bottle of wine you mentioned last night? And two glasses."

We spent the rest of the day in front of the fire, talking as the wind whipped outside and rain lashed the floor-to-ceiling windows, catching up on the past five years—with one major omission.

I encouraged Alex to talk about himself—his plane, his wild-child brother and scholarly college-aged sister, his life and duties as a prince. For some reason he seemed fascinated by my mundane life as well, asking endless questions about AJ, my business, my friends, and my stepmother and stepsisters.

"I can't believe you're employing them. I remember you saying you'd never met two more entitled, lazy, selfish girls. I always thought they were complete brats. I hope they've changed."

I laughed and took another sip of the delicious white wine. "Not exactly. Well, I guess they're too old to be brats now."

"But the other adjectives?"

I laughed again. "If the shoe fits... Anyway, I like my work. It's fulfilling to help other people, and more importantly, it pays the bills for AJ and me. The hours are a bit longer than I'd like, but we all have to work, right?"

Then I snickered and executed a bow with an overly elaborate hand flourish. "Well, unless we're born into *royalty*."

"It's not all it's cracked up to be. Believe me, I *work*. It's just not the kind of work I'd prefer to do."

"What would you rather do, if you weren't too busy *prince-ing*, that is."

Alex chuckled at the made-up word but then got serious. "I'd be a full-time pilot, travel the world, go where I wanted to go and do what I wanted to do instead of being controlled by duty. How about you? What if you could do anything? Would you still run your cleaning company?"

I thought about it a moment. "I wouldn't want to dissolve it and let my clients down. But honestly? If money were no concern, I'd turn the day-to-day running of it over to someone else and spend a lot more time with AJ. I've never told anyone this, but... I'd even kind of like to homeschool him. Does that sound crazy?"

"Not at all. My siblings and I were all homeschooled—well, we had tutors who came to the palace—but it's a brilliant way to do things... leaves a lot more time and opportunity for travel."

There was a gleam in Alex's eye I didn't necessarily like, but he moved on to other topics, and I happily answered his questions about AJ's favorite activities, toys, and friends.

I told him about my son's favorite teacher at preschool, a young woman named Angelina whose gentle demeanor and long platinum locks fit her name perfectly.

"AJ wants to marry her when he grows up," I informed Alex. "I've given my blessing, though she says she plans to be a nun."

"An actual nun? As in a habit-wearing, no-marriage-or-love-life nun?"

"Yep. She says that's what she's always planned to do with her life."

"Well, I guess she's not an option then, but he'll find the right girl one day," Alex said. "Though sometimes, the first one to move into your heart simply refuses to vacate the premises."

For a moment we held searing eye contact. My own heart squeezed almost to the point of bursting, but I chose to ignore the palpable tension.

And his loaded remark about first loves.

"Are you hungry? I'm starved. What do we have around here for dinner?" I asked.

Instead of pushing the subject, Alex dropped it. "Let me go see. Want me to help you to the kitchen? You could sit at the island and keep me company while I attempt to work culinary wonders with crackers, tuna, and jarred peppers."

"Sure."

Alex put on a shirt (unfortunately) then helped me hobble to one of the bar stools and get up on it. With one hand, I clung to his arm for support. With the other, I clutched the front of the robe to prevent the two flaps of fabric from parting and flashing him.

As he prepared the food, Alex continued to ask about AJ. "What kind of baby was he?"

"Not every minute was perfect, of course, but he was easy compared to most babies," I said, picturing my son's cherubic baby face.

"I have a friend whose daughter cried every naptime and bedtime until she was three. When I'd put AJ down for the night, he smiled up at me and closed his eyes. I was almost embarrassed to tell people he started sleeping through the night at three months."

"That must have made his father happy."

My ease vanished. Alex was fishing again. I could tell by his tone of voice.

"He was already gone by then."

"Idiot," Alex muttered to the bowl in front of him, then more loudly he asked, "What happened with you two? Why did you break up? I can't imagine what would make a man abandon his newborn, not to mention a woman like you."

An attack of nerves made my hands shake to the point I had to put them in my lap to hide it.

"I'm not used to talking about him," I said cryptically. "I'd really rather not."

Alex was clearly not thrilled at my evasion but nodded his agreement, still looking angry as he turned around and set a dinner plate in front of me.

"I'll say this one more thing... whatever happened... he was a fool to let you go. And I certainly hope he never develops the balls to show has face again, demanding some kind of parental rights."

You and me both, sweet prince. You and me both.

TWENTY

Rainbows on Demand

Alex

Jealousy was eating me alive.

Though I knew it was ridiculous, though I knew Cinda's life hadn't simply frozen in place the minute I left America, it killed me to think of her with another man.

To know that *he* was out there, somewhere, and that one day he'd come to his senses and return to reclaim her and his child.

It was inevitable. No one could be stupid enough to walk away from this woman for good.

Once upon a time I had been certain *I'd* be the one to father her children. But I'd left, and some other man had claimed the honor. As much as I'd like to, I didn't own her.

I worked to suppress the envy I felt for this unnamed, absent *fool* of a man and focused on taking care of Cinda. I did everything I could think of to make her comfortable, kept up with her pain reliever doses, prepared whatever meals I could scrape together from the non-perishables that had been left at the house, and monitored the weather updates on the radio.

For most of the day, the gale continued to howl outside, the rain pelting the windowpanes like pebbles.

As far as I was concerned, the wind could pick up the house and set us down in Oz. I was with Cinda again, and it was the only place in the world I wanted to be.

The warmth and soft, orangey glow from the fireplace made the room feel like the safest place on earth, and I felt a sense of contentment I hadn't felt in oh... five years or so.

At one point in the evening—I couldn't be sure what time because the power was still out, and both our phones were dead—the storm moved off-shore.

Standing at the window, I could still see the rain falling over the water and the ocean churning beneath the dark clouds, but rays of late day sun made an appearance.

Before long, the combination of the lingering precipitation and the setting sun created a magnificent rainbow. It seemed to stretch from one end of the island to the other.

I practically ran to the couch where Cinda was reading and swept her up in my arms, cradle style. "You've got to see this."

Cinda had always been in love with rainbows. I'd seen her literally dance with happiness once when one had appeared over the beach club.

"What is it?" She asked as we moved toward the door to the back porch.

"You'll see. Can you reach the doorknob there? Yeah? Good."

She let go of her robe long enough to pull the door ajar. I kicked it the rest of the way open and carried her out onto the porch. The rainbow was even more vibrant, now joined by a dazzling sunset. I'd never seen anything more beautiful.

Until I turned and looked at Cinda's face.

The glow in her eyes was more than an effect of the remarkable natural light show. It came from within, and it was proof positive the girl I'd loved was still there, just a bit older and even more breathtaking.

God, there was nothing better in this world than making her happy.

"Didn't I tell you?" I said softly.

She nodded, looking almost too astonished to speak. "It's… incredible. Talk about the calm after the storm." Now her gaze shifted to meet mine. "Thank you, Alex."

The combination of her sweet smile and hearing my voice in that familiar, sweetly indulgent tone made me feel like I'd swallowed a few beams of the late day sun.

"You're welcome. Cooking, porter service, rainbows on demand—we aim to please."

She laughed. "You're still just as goofy as you used to be."

"True, unfortunately." A long pause. "And you're still just as lovely."

Darting her eyes away, Cinda squirmed in my arms, clearly uncomfortable. "I must be getting heavy. I'd suggest putting me down on the bench so we could keep watching the sunset, but it's soaking wet."

"No worries," I said. "I'll take you back inside and dry the bench off with some bath towels. Then we can come back out and stay until dark."

"Okay."

I carried her back into the house, intending to leave her on the sofa until I'd gotten the bench seat dried off. But as I set her down on the cushions, the bounce caused our foreheads to collide with an audible thunk.

"Ow," we said in unison then laughed together.

The laughter faded as the eye contact between us stretched out and became more intense. Both of us remained absolutely still except for our rapid breathing, which sounded loud in the quiet room.

The sparks firing between our bodies were almost visible. I

certainly felt them. Slowly, very slowly, I leaned forward and pressed my lips to her forehead. Her skin was sweet, slightly damp, and oh so tempting.

Oh you are *a goner, aren't you? Turned on by a forehead kiss? Pathetic.*

Pulling back, I checked Cinda's expression.

"Is that better?" I asked, nearly breathless.

She nodded, her eyes wide and dark. Their focus dropped to my lips. Encouraged, I leaned in again. This time my target was her mouth. Every nerve was strung tight as I braced for her rebuff.

It didn't come.

Our lips met, and raw emotion charged through me as Cinda returned my kiss.

Yes. Yes, yes, yes.

As our mouths moved together, her fingers sank into my hair and caressed my nape. Currents of electric pleasure crackled under my skin, and all my muscles felt swollen as my whole body flooded with adrenaline.

Tugging at the hem of my shirt, she urged it up and over my head.

"Wow," she said on a breathy exhale then went right back to exploring my neck, shoulders, and chest with her hands as we kissed ravenously.

Finally—*finally*—the moment I'd been imagining nonstop since running into her at the mansion was happening. It was better than I'd dreamed, maybe even better than it had been all those years ago.

And it made one thing crystal clear—Cinda was everything I'd been missing and feared I'd never have again.

My passion for life hadn't disappeared after all. It was still there, as strong as ever. It had simply been lying dormant these past few years, waiting to be reawakened by the inexplicable power of this one small woman.

When her tormenting fingers slid down over my ribs to stroke the tense muscles of my abdomen, carnal urgency exploded through my body. That's when I lost *all* ability to control my need to touch *her*.

My hands roamed greedily, moving over her hair, her shoulders and back then delving inside her gaping oversized robe. All the while I kissed her like she was the only source of oxygen in the universe.

For me, she was. I realized I'd been getting by on life support all these years, never taking a full, satisfying breath, merely surviving instead of really living.

Exerting pressure on my nape and lower back, Cinda pulled me down to her until I joined her on the couch. The pleasure of the full-body contact made me dizzy, and the sweet, needy sounds she made were driving me fucking wild.

As I settled my hardness more deeply into her welcoming soft curves, it occurred to me belatedly I might be hurting her.

I lifted my head. "Is your ankle all right?"

"What ankle?" Cinda whispered before locking her mouth with mine again. She gripped my shoulders and arched her back, rubbing herself against the ridge of my erection.

Excellent. She was just as into this as I was, apparently just as consumed by the same brand of insanity, pent-up desire that had finally burgeoned past its boundaries.

Still, I reached behind me and drew her knee upward, carefully propping the injured ankle on the sofa's cushioned spine, out of harm's way.

Which left her legs enticingly splayed.

Breaking contact with her lips, I kissed a path to her ear then down her neck and chest to the fragrant skin between her breasts. The inner curves of them were exposed where the robe parted. I pushed it open just as the final rays of sunset shone through the window on us.

The warm light fell on her naked skin, gilding her beautiful breasts with a golden glow and bringing to mind that proverbial pot of gold.

A chuckle in my throat joined a groan of desire.

A treasure, indeed.

And it was all *mine*.

Though I had no right to make the claim, Cinda *was* mine — I felt it down to my bones. No matter where she went or who she was with, whether we were in the same room or a world apart, she was mine and always would be.

Mine to protect, mine to comfort.

Mine to claim.

And that's what I would do. I couldn't stop myself any longer.

TWENTY-ONE
I Remember You

Cinda

This was such a mistake.

And yet, I was going to make it—and no doubt enjoy every second of it. Somewhere between the rainbow sunset and that mind-scrambling kiss, I'd lost every ounce of willpower I possessed.

I was simply unable to resist Alex any longer.

It had been forever since someone had kissed me, touched me, made me feel good. More than that, it was *him*—everything about him.

Not only was he sweet, and smart and funny, he was ridiculously good looking with his tousled raven hair, sun-glazed skin, and huge, powerfully muscled form looming above me.

He was also unbelievably good with his hands.

And his mouth.

That beautiful full-lipped mouth royal watchers obsessed over on social media worldwide.

Yes, I'd checked out the articles—and the zillions of drool-worthy photos they posted—once I found out his real name.

The fangirls and fanboys weren't wrong. Those lips looked like they were made for sin. They felt even better.

The *way* he *kissed* me. Gah!

Alex had been sexy five years ago. Now... he was a god. And I was a willing sacrifice.

Just this once. That was all I could afford. But I would cling to every touch, every minute of this one time with him and make the memory of it last for a lifetime.

Already it was unforgettable.

Spread out before him like some kind of raunchy men's magazine centerfold, I couldn't even dredge up any shame or modesty. I was too turned on by the look of utter desire on his face.

"You're so beautiful," he said in a whisper that sounded almost reverential. "I've always thought so. But now... my God..."

It was obvious he was ready—I could see it, and I could *feel* it in the waves of heat pouring from his body, the barely suppressed energy charging beneath his flushed skin. But he took his time.

Lowering his mouth to my breast, he browsed over it, skimming the taut nipple with the flat of his tongue before pulling it fully into his mouth and licking in swirls of maddening sensation while he cupped and kneaded the softness.

My fingers tangled in his silky hair while my body undulated in pleading pulses. "Alex," I panted. "I want you. It's been so long."

I reached for the waistband of his shorts, which was already pushed away from his abdomen thanks to the glorious hard-on he was sporting.

That's for me. It was hard to keep myself from clapping.

Instead, I ran my hand over the outside of the nylon shorts, refamiliarizing myself with the impressive length of him before delving beneath the fabric to touch the satiny hardness.

Alex groaned, and his fingers encircled my wrist, removing my hand from his pants.

"It's been a long time for me, too." His chuckle was a regretful sound. "Which means it's too soon for *that*."

He kissed away my pout then pushed my arms over my head so I could no longer reach him.

"Let me have my way with you Cinda," he whispered. "I've literally dreamed about it a thousand times."

I shivered and nodded, feeling like I was dreaming myself yet more fully alive than I'd been in years. Every part of me was swollen and tingling, waiting for his skillful attention.

Teasing the tips of my uplifted breasts with his tongue, he moved lower, forging a trail of fire down my torso to my navel and then south of it. He spread my legs even wider with his hands then sifted through the intimate curls, humming in apparent appreciation for what he found.

With gentle deliberateness, he pressed his mouth against me in a wet, open-mouthed kiss that made it impossible for me to think or even breathe. My one good foot ground into the floor beside the couch, and all my muscles tightened as I arched upward into the pleasure, driven by an eternal need to get closer to him.

Alex kissed and licked and taunted and soothed until I was in a frenzy. Bowing my back and rocking upward, I brought my hands to the sides of his head and curled my fingers into the heavy locks of his hair.

Which I hoped I didn't pull out of his scalp because *holy hell* this was intense.

Oh God. Oh God, Alex.

My hips bucked in frantic thrusts as I groaned and ground against his tongue, calling his name.

And then I was silent for a long moment because apparently I was dying—no, actually, not dying, just on pleasure overload that short-circuited my brain for a second. I was decidedly *not* silent after that, crying out helplessly and thrashing in a way that would probably mortify me later when I was capable of rational thought.

Limp with satisfaction, I dragged my fingernails through Alex's messy hair and over his shoulders, watching chill bumps rise on the smooth surface.

"Come here," I murmured, and he obligingly crawled up my body. His smile was nothing less than triumphant as his face hovered over mine.

"I remember you," I purred.

"And I remember you. But you taste even better than I remembered."

He nuzzled into the space below my ear, and then his mouth found mine. Alex kissed me fiercely, the strokes deep, almost punishing, and I felt his body trembling.

Stroking my hands over his back and lean sides, I hooked my thumbs into his waistband and pushed his shorts from his hips. His erection sprang free, rigid and pulsing and ready to give me what I'd been missing desperately all these years.

He hissed and dropped his head back on his shoulders, looking heavenward as I wrapped my hand around the hot length. I urged him toward me, but he resisted, staring down at me with half-lidded eyes full of fire and mystery and promise.

"What are you waiting for?" I whispered.

TWENTY-TWO
Duty

Alex

The soft skin of Cinda's inner thighs bracketed my hips, and her scent was all around me. The heat of her sweet center, mere inches away, beckoned to me.

I hovered there, at the precipice of heaven, wanting to preserve every detail of this moment—her parted, kiss-swollen mouth, her shimmering blue eyes, her golden hair spread out on the sofa cushion and spilling over the side.

There was no one in this world like her, and no one had ever made me feel like this.

No one but her ever could.

After all the years of missing her, of longing and fantasizing and lying to myself that I would get over it, we were about to be one again.

And *this*—this was how it was meant to be.

The difference between this relationship—tangled and uncertain as it was—and the impersonal, political marriage I was expected to share with Audrey deRamel was night and day.

Oh shit. *Audrey.*

The unwanted reality of my life intruded on the intimate moment like an out of control vehicle crashing through a storefront.

Even then my muscles trembled with the struggle *not* to drive forward and bury myself in the only place I wanted to be.

The last thing I wanted to do was stop—I felt like I could spend every moment for the rest of my life making love to Cinda.

But I forced myself to pull back before I lost all awareness of anything outside this room and this incredible woman beneath me.

The fact was life *did* exist outside this room. Audrey existed. I was within a couple of days of being engaged to her.

My family and my duty existed, and they weren't just going to vanish into thin air.

Duty. I'd had the attribute drilled into me since I could first understand the meaning of the word. Right now I despised even the sound of it.

Because another word had moved to the forefront of my mind. Love.

Did I still love Cinda?

Just being in the same room with her was like rain after a drought. As we'd spoken throughout the day, her voice had sunk into my pores, quenching a thirst I hadn't realized the severity of until now.

I felt *full* with her around. I felt complete. I felt like... myself.

How had I lived all these years without her? How would I go *on* living when I had to leave this place?

That's what duty would require. It demanded that I keep my promise to my father about joining our family with Audrey's. It demanded I go back to Aubernesse and someday rule there—with a suitable bride by my side.

But I'd made promises to Cinda too—years ago. Did she still remember them?

Would she still even want what I'd promised?

For a moment we just stared into each other's eyes, both breathing fast and audibly.

"Are you okay?" she whispered, sliding her hand around to my lower back and nudging me closer again in an unmistakable invitation I was desperate to accept.

But I couldn't. Not tonight.

I nodded. "Yeah. I'm great." Brushing the hair back from her face, I dragged the tip of my finger down her nose to her plush, kiss-swollen lips.

She opened them and sucked my finger inside, causing a groan to escape me and my cock to launch an all-out protest against the travesty I was about to commit.

"But I think we should wait..." *And I can't tell you why.* A brainstorm hit me with the perfect excuse. "...unless you have a stash of condoms in that cleaning kit of yours?"

She half-laughed, half-groaned. "No. I don't. You'd be surprised how few orgies occur during house-cleaning jobs."

"I'm pleased to hear it." I chuckled.

Cinda collapsed back and rolled her eyes then covered her flushed face with one hand.

"I'm so embarrassed. I can't believe I wasn't even *thinking* about protection. You must think I'm an idiot or at least totally irresponsible."

"I definitely don't think you're an idiot. And you shouldn't be embarrassed."

Truth be told, I hadn't been thinking about protection either. I was only using the lack of condoms as a cover story.

"I don't think you're irresponsible either. I am perfectly willing to believe you were so overwhelmed by my amazing lovemaking skills that your mind was too frazzled to think of practical matters."

"It's true actually," Cinda said, wearing a rueful grin. "You are..." She let out a little sigh. "Very, very good at it."

She reached for my cock again, but I rocked my hips back and pushed up to one knee, snagging my shorts from the floor and pulling them on.

Cinda watched me, wearing a look of shock. "But you didn't... you don't want me to...?"

She shot a meaningful look at the bulge in the front of my shorts.

Yes. Fuck yes. I winced, as my frustrated body gave my responsible brain a swift kick in the ass.

"Believe me... I'd love nothing more," I told her honestly. 'But I don't trust myself around you. If we went any farther... well, you remember what happened when we were young. I'm not sure I'm any better at controlling myself with you now then I was back then. I could have gotten you pregnant several times over."

My brain seized on that image. Cinda big and pregnant with my child. The mental picture produced a longing so sudden and powerful it rocked me to my core.

It wasn't helping with that massive hard-on either.

She, however, heeded my warning, restoring her robe and cinching it with the belt, removing all that cream-and-pink skin from view. Only then did my dick admit defeat and vow to return and fight another day.

Cinda had gotten quiet. She glanced at me with a look that was unaccountably shy considering the intimacies we'd just shared.

"If you're worried about, you know... diseases or whatever, don't be. It's true what I said. I haven't been with anyone since—"

She cut herself off, but I finished the sentence for her. "Since AJ's dad?"

"Yes," she said softly.

Jealousy lit a quick-moving brush fire in my gut. "A hard act to follow, huh? He was that good?"

"Actually, yes."

"I hate him," I said, only partially joking.

"I did, too," she confessed. "For a long time. But not anymore. We were both young and stupid."

I snorted. "Sounds familiar. But look at you now. You've had to be so strong for so long, doing it all alone. You're a remarkable woman, Cinda. And I know you're a wonderful mother. AJ is lucky to have you."

I wish I could.

"Thank you," she whispered, her eyes glistening with unshed tears.

Draping an arm around her shoulders, I pulled her against my chest and kissed the top of her head.

She was stiff at first for some reason but eventually snuggled into me, wrapping her arm around my stomach and waist and staring ahead at the low-burning fire while I glided a hand over her head and shoulders in soothing, repetitive strokes.

She was quiet for so long I thought she might have fallen asleep, but then I heard her soft voice.

"Whatever happens after this, I'm glad we had this time together. It helps me, knowing the truth about what happened... that I wasn't in it alone, that I didn't imagine your feelings for me back then."

After a pause she added, "I'm glad you're still you. I missed you, Alex."

A giant hand reached into my chest and squeezed my heart, stealing my breath for a second.

How could the same woman who'd groaned and writhed under my tongue just minutes ago also be so sweet? She absolutely slayed me.

My hand on her shoulder squeezed. "I missed you, too."

The words seemed inane—and completely inadequate. But I wasn't free to say more—not yet.

I never wanted to leave this spot, but at the same time, I was eager to return to the mainland and get my life straightened out so I could finally say all the things I wanted to say to Cinda.

"I'm scheduled to fly back to Aubernesse Sunday after the ball," I told her.

She nodded against my chest. "I know. One of my crews is supposed to clean the house Monday."

"Before I go... I'd..."

I shouldn't say it. I knew better. What good could it possibly lead to? But I found myself finishing the thought. "I'd like to meet your son... if you'll allow it."

She lifted her head. A strange look crossed her face. It was almost like apprehension. "Why?"

"Because he's a huge part of your life. He's part of *you.* And if he's anything like you, I know I'll love him."

Because I still love you.

And there it was. The L word. I didn't say it aloud. There were some things I needed to take care of before I was at liberty to make that confession.

But there was no point in denying it to myself any longer.

Loving Cinda was something I had no more control over than that miraculous sunset we'd watched or the wind and rain that had come before it.

* * *

Claiming she was tired, Cinda went to sleep shortly after total darkness fell.

Just like the previous night, I barely slept. I was way too keyed up from the day. Even with all the conversation and revelations, I still felt like I'd missed so much that I never wanted to sleep again.

Instead, I watched her sleep. She was the most beautiful thing I'd ever seen—even more so than she'd been years ago.

Alternating waves of gratitude and disbelief washed over me as I listened to her soft breaths and gazed at her peaceful face, convincing myself she was real and not some vivid dream born out of too many years of wanting and not having.

It was physically painful to be this close to her without touching her. Several times I was tempted to sneak over to her side of the room and wake her with a kiss.

Of course I didn't. What would she do if she woke to find me there, nuzzling her soft hair and breathing in its light perfume? Kissing the sweet curve of her cheek? Caressing the silky skin that had driven me to distraction?

Tell me to get lost? Or worse, welcome me with open arms and invite me to share her bed?

The front of my shorts tented again, my ever-hopeful dick assuring me it was ready for action if I was.

Whoa there big guy. Better turn that ship around before you run into the rocks.

I fought to regain control of my charging thoughts, to remind myself how tenuous it all was. It was foolish to get so emotionally invested when I had no idea how she felt about me now.

Though we'd kissed—and gone pretty fucking far *beyond* kissing—Cinda had given me no indication she had any lingering feelings for me beyond the obvious physical attraction we shared.

Our lives were literally a world apart. Hers was filled with family and friends on this continent, a business she'd built from scratch… and a son.

We'd both have to go home tomorrow. Beyond that? Well, I just didn't know.

We hadn't talked about the future. We'd just barely begun discussing the past. But deep in my soul, a new certainty had taken root. What had happened between us years ago *had* been the real thing, and that wasn't something that came along very often.

She was the love of my life, and now she was back *in* my life. I'd found her at long last. That had to mean something.

It wasn't a sure thing, but there *might* be a future for us. The idea filled me with a sense of anticipation reminiscent of my childhood days waiting for Father Christmas to arrive with Cam and Janey.

In fact, I was looking forward to the future in a way I hadn't in a long, long time. I'd discovered what was missing from my life, and now that I'd found her, I would never let Cinda go again.

If I could've had my wish, I would have gotten down on one knee that very night and asked her the question I'd never gotten the chance to ask years ago. But there were some matters I had to address first, and I intended to do that the minute we arrived back on the mainland.

One, decency demanded that I inform my intended fiancée the deal was off. Second, and this one would be more difficult, I'd have to talk to my family.

I had a feeling they wouldn't react well to the abrupt change of plans, but it didn't really matter. Some things were more important than duty and tradition.

I only hoped that after all was said and done... Cinda would agree.

TWENTY-THREE
Someone I'd Like You to Meet

Cinda—Friday

My ankle was much better, but I was still limping as Alex helped me out of the terminal at Eastport Bay's airport.

He'd wanted Jorge the cab driver to take us to the Block Island Medical Center that morning, but I'd refused, promising him I'd be fine and would go to my own doctor in Eastport Bay if I felt it was necessary.

Finally, he'd relented but insisted I allow him to fly me home. Knowing it would be more comfortable on my ankle than a bouncy boat ride and would get me back sooner—before AJ got out of school at three—I accepted the offer.

Power had been restored on the island late that morning, and we'd both gotten just enough charge on our phones to text and let everyone know we were safe and on our way back. I'd texted Kristal first.

Cinda: Flying home at noon with Alex instead of taking ferry. Will catch a cab. Dying to see you and AJ!

I would save the details for later when we spoke in person. There was so much to say. And I wanted to get my best friend's take on when—and how—to tell Alex the truth.

I still wasn't sure it was the smartest thing to let him see my son, though he'd asked to and I had new reasons to hope for a reconciliation.

One thing *was* for sure—I wasn't ready yet. I needed more time to prepare—and gather the courage.

Scanning the parking lot, Alex said, "Don't take a cab. My driver will be happy to take you home."

"The prince has a royal chauffeur?" I said playfully. "How posh. Your life is unbelievable. It's like something out of a movie."

He grinned. "Don't worry. You'll get used to it."

There it was again, the implication that today was not the end of our reunion but a new beginning. Looking up at his handsome face, I doubted I could *ever* get used to all the amazing things a life with him would entail.

But I wanted the opportunity to find out.

Yes, I had to admit it. Despite my fears, despite the risk, despite my longstanding policy of never allowing myself to count on a man... I wanted Alex in my life. And in AJ's life.

Over the past two days, I'd been struck again and again by the power of my feelings for Alex. It felt like the five-year separation hadn't happened at all, love rushing right back in to fill the hollow spots like a tide coming in and covering the contours of the rocky shoreline of Eastport Bay.

Though we'd shared unexpected intimacies, he hadn't said he still loved *me*, hadn't made any promises. It was too soon for all that. But my heart soared with hope, rivaling the private plane flight we'd shared from the island.

As we waited on the sidewalk, Alex kept a supporting arm around me. I felt him looking at me nearly non-stop.

I had on zero makeup and had let my hair dry naturally, lacking any styling tools or products at the beach house. In other words, I was a complete mess.

Embarrassed, I glanced up and met his eyes. "Why are you staring at me? You're making me self-conscious."

"I just can't get over the fact that you're really here, that yesterday actually happened. I love hurricanes by the way," Alex said, squeezing me more tightly. "Big, big fan."

I laughed. "That one had its charm, I guess. At least we won't easily forget the experience."

"I won't forget a minute of it. These past two days have been some of the best in my life."

"Really?" I wrinkled my nose in disbelief. "Even without power?"

"I don't need electric shavers and coffeemakers to be happy." His carefree demeanor dropped suddenly, his eyes focusing on mine with weighty intent. "All I need is you. I hope you feel the same."

I was struck by a dizzying sense of unreality. Between the bizarre circumstances of our reunion and the muscle relaxant, the storm, and the magical rainbow that had signaled its end, our time on the island together had felt like a dream.

And now Alex was declaring himself to me in an airport parking lot.

"This feels almost too good to be true, you and me here together. Feeling your arms around me. You're not going to vanish on me again, are you?" I asked.

"Never. I promise." Alex punctuated his answer with a sweet kiss that reached down to my very soul.

It *felt* like a promise—that he *would* be there for me, that I could count on him, that we could be a real family.

"I do have to fly home on Sunday to take care of some state business," he said. "But I'll come right back. I want to see you as much as possible. And I want a chance to meet—"

He was interrupted by the sound of a child's excited voice.

"Mommy! Mommy, we came to get you."

Recognizing it instantly, I whirled around.

Oh no.

AJ and Kristal were in the mostly deserted parking lot, standing beside the new Mercedes G Wagon Hunter had insisted on buying for Kristal. The rambunctious four-year-old was trying to squirm out of her grip and get to me.

What were they doing here? Had Kristal misunderstood my text and taken it as an invitation to come to the airport?

Sweat popped out at the roots of my hair, and my stomach fell to the dusty gray pavement.

Well, it was too late now. My child was eager to greet me, and I wasn't going to let him see how much his unexpected presence was complicating my life.

Conscious of Alex's watchful gaze, I stepped off the curb and started making my way toward my son, who'd succeeded in escaping Kristal.

"AJ," I cried, holding out my arms to him. "Oh my goodness, little bear, I'm so happy to see you. I thought you'd be in school right now."

He flew at me, grabbing me around the knees and squeezing hard. "Kris-thal said you were coming home on a airplane, and I wanted to pick you up at the airport, and she said it would be okay to miss school for one day and surprise you."

"He begged," Kristal added. "It's his superpower."

"Of course, it's okay." Moving slowly to accommodate my tender ankle, I dropped to my knees and wrapped AJ in my arms, burying my nose in his silky, dark, clean-smelling hair. "What a great surprise. Mommy missed you so much."

Drawing back, I said, "Look at you—I think you've gotten taller since I saw you two days ago."

He nodded vigorously. "I have. And Kris-thal and me made even more slime, and I'm not scared of storms anymore."

"Wow. You really have grown up then."

Alex moved in my peripheral vision. He'd followed me across the parking lot, probably trying to make sure I didn't fall on my face.

Had he gotten a look at AJ yet? My stomach and head swam simultaneously. If he hadn't yet, it was only a matter of seconds.

Kristal stepped forward and introduced herself, extending her hand over my head.

"Hi Alex. It's nice to finally meet you."

"You too. You've heard of me then?"

Kristal rolled her eyes. "For years."

Darting a glance at me, she raised a sardonic brow. "Looks like you two managed to find some common ground. I was so happy when I got Cinda's text that you were flying home *together*."

Based on her giddy tone, Kristal had obviously seen us kiss and assumed we were a couple again.

I wondered if AJ had noticed it too. He'd never seen me so much as hold hands with a man. What must be going through his mind?

If he learned Alex was a real live prince, my son would start planning the wedding right then and there.

I'd hoped for a little more time to plan how to introduce them, how to explain things to AJ—and to Alex.

But it was too late for that. Here they both were. My stomach did a crazy flip, anticipating the monumental moment.

Rising to my feet, I turned toward Alex. The look on his face nearly stopped my heart. He stared at AJ, his jaw slack, his brown eyes wide, a whirlwind of thoughts behind them.

He knows.

Grappling for my son's small hand, I swallowed hard and forced myself to speak without stuttering. "AJ, buddy, there's someone I'd like for you to meet."

Before I could say any more, AJ dropped my hand and stepped forward. He looked Alex straight in the eye, his little face very serious.

"You're the man who made my mommy work all day and night."

Alex got down on one knee, putting the two of them at eye level with each other. I went breathless observing them, their profiles so similar it made my heart ache.

I had never expected to witness this moment. Now that it was happening, it was nearly impossible to hold the tears at bay. I didn't want to alarm AJ though, so I fought them.

Alex extended a hand toward his mini-me son, matching his somber expression. "Very sorry about that. I'm Alexander Wessex. You can call me Alex."

AJ's eyes popped, and he turned to me with a big smile then faced Alex again, taking his offered hand and pumping his arm a couple of times.

"We have the same name. I'm Alexander Joseph Brown. You can call me AJ."

Well, *if* Alex hadn't figured it out by looking at the child, there could be no more doubt in his mind now. I'd named AJ after him. My son's middle name, Joseph, was in honor of my late father.

Alex looked up at me in astonishment. His gaze went back to AJ then returned to me, tears glistening in his eyes.

A mixture of joy and absolute terror filled my heart, warring until I was afraid the combatants would break through its battered walls.

Sounding like he was choking back tears, Alex returned his full attention to AJ. "That is... that's a very fine name. I'm pleased to meet you, AJ."

"Are you a pilot?" AJ was clearly excited by the prospect. My son loved anything that flew. Planes were his absolute favorite.

"I am," Alex said. "Would you like to fly in my plane sometime?"

AJ nodded, his wispy brows raised high and a grin on his face.

"I could even teach you to fly if you'd like," Alex offered.

At that, I walked over and interrupted. We were getting ahead of ourselves. It would be a long time before I'd feel comfortable enough to let my son board a plane with Alex.

Planes flew overseas, to places like Aubernesse where Alex and his family had complete and total jurisdiction and I had no rights whatsoever.

Alex and I needed to talk—a lot—and figure out where our relationship stood before getting AJ involved. At the moment I was too discombobulated to string two sentences together.

"We'll have to see about that." I took AJ's hand. "Hey—who wants some ice cream?"

"Me!" AJ began hopping with enthusiasm. "Can we get some right now?"

"Sure. Let's go. Say goodbye to the pilot now."

"Can he come with us to get ice cream?" AJ begged.

"Not today, buddy. Another time maybe. Alex, it was nice... seeing you. Thank you for getting me home safely."

I turned to walk away with my son, but Alex snagged my sleeve. "Cinda... I'd like to speak with you for a moment—privately."

Nerves bubbled to the top of my stomach.

He wasn't going to let me escape so easily.

TWENTY-FOUR
Not What You Think It Is

Cinda

Turning to Kristal, I said, "Would you mind taking AJ to the car? I'll be right there."

I bent down to speak to my son. "Mommy needs to speak to Alex for one minute, and then we'll go home, okay?"

AJ sounded distressed. "I want to have ice cream with the pilot."

"It's okay, buddy." I faked a lightness I didn't feel. "We'll go get ice cream together this afternoon—just you and me."

Kristal placed a supportive hand on my shoulder, giving it a squeeze, then led AJ away as he dragged his feet and wailed, "But I want to go on the plaaaane."

If there was one hard and fast rule of parenthood, it was that your child was guaranteed to throw a tantrum at the worst possible place and time.

When he was out of earshot, I girded myself and turned back to Alex. His face was flushed a dark red. His eyes looked almost crazed.

He was not taking this well. He was beyond surprised.

He was *furious.*

"How old is he?" he demanded in a deadly quiet voice.

I didn't answer. I looked down at my feet, willing myself to keep breathing.

Wrapping his fingers around my upper arm, Alex turned me to face him again. "Cinda... *how old* is your son?"

My gaze flickered up to his then down again. I licked my lips, and I could feel myself trembling all over.

"He's four. And a half—almost."

"Four and a half," Alex repeated in a papery voice. He looked shell-shocked.

"He's yours, Alex," I said quietly, admitting the obvious. "I'm sure you've figured that out already."

He nodded over and over again, breathing as if he'd completed a half-marathon. Finally, he spoke, his voice a gaunt whisper.

"I have a son."

"Yes. You do. We do. I didn't tell you earlier because—"

Alex cut me off, his voice stronger now. The words snapped like a whip. "I have a *son* I knew nothing about."

Before I could respond, a shiny black Rolls Royce pulled up to the curb. The car stopped, and a man got out. He was heavyset and balding with thick gray eyebrows.

Coming around the back of the car, he approached Alex, wearing a wide, oblivious smile.

"So good to see you safe and sound, Your Highness. Your parents have been worried sick."

"Still in one piece," Alex assured him. His smile was unbearably tight, his voice formal. "Patton, may I introduce Cinda Brown? We're old friends. We were stranded on the island together."

Patton smiled warmly and offered his hand. "So nice to meet you, Miss Brown. Glad you made it through safely as well. That was some storm, huh?"

I made my tone as polite and unaffected as possible in spite of the conspicuous tension in the air.

"It was. We're lucky it wasn't worse."

Glancing back to Alex, the man said, "The mansion is fine. And you'll be happy to hear that your fiancée and her parents finally made it in. They had some delays, but I picked them up at T.F. Green this morning and drove them to the mansion."

Beside me, Alex froze.

So did my heart, turning to pure ice and shattering an instant later. Then it flash-broiled as the driver's words sank in.

It was a struggle to breathe, much less speak, but after a few seconds I managed to shift my focus to Alex.

His face said it all.

"What is he talking about Alex? What fiancée?"

I wasn't even sure why I'd asked the question. His answer didn't matter. What mattered was that he'd once again failed to be up front with me.

Just as he had almost five years earlier, he'd chosen to omit information that was vitally important.

"It's not what you think it is."

"I'm pretty sure I know what the word fiancée means," I bit out. "I may be a fool but I'm not stupid."

What had the past few days even been about? Why had he kissed me and said all those tender things about being so happy I was back in his life?

Was he expecting me to be his *mistress* or something?

"Patton, would you excuse us please?" Alex said.

The chauffeur quick-stepped back around the car and slid into the driver's seat, shutting the door firmly behind him.

Alex moved toward me, reaching out. I recoiled from his touch, stumbling backward.

"It's not what it seems," he said. "It's an arranged marriage. I don't even know the woman."

"But you *have* agreed to marry her." My heart thrashed in my chest as I awaited confirmation.

"Yes, but—"

"My son is waiting for me."

Turning my back to Alex, I marched away toward the SUV where Kristal and AJ waited with the engine running.

Well, it was more of a limp than a march, but the attitude was the same.

I'd known better than to allow myself to entertain the idea of relying on someone. This was no more than what I'd expected.

Through the vehicle's rolled-up windows, I could hear my son crying. I felt like falling apart too, but I would not—*would not*—allow myself to do it.

Not until I was alone.

Alex jogged after me. "Cinda, wait. I can explain."

I didn't turn around, just kept up my hobbled pace. "We were together in that house for two days. *Two days.* You had plenty of time to explain, and you didn't even mention the fact that you're engaged to be *married*?"

"I'm not, though," Alex said. "I mean, yes, for all practical purposes I am engaged to be engaged. But it won't become official until the ball tomorrow night. I didn't mention it because I needed some time to take care of things, to speak with my family. And to Audrey."

Audrey. It was even worse now that she had a name.

This was real. It was happening. Any fantasies I might have concocted about a reconciliation with Alex evaporated in an instant.

Whether AJ spotted me and recognized my distress, or he was just still in the throes of his tantrum, he cried even louder.

Which didn't help Alex's case.

At all.

"Please, Cinda, listen to me," Alex pleaded.

I whirled to face him, placing a staying hand on his chest. "No, you listen to me. Hurting me is one thing—hurting my child is something totally different. And I'm not going to give you the chance to do it. We don't need your weak explanations, or your *omitted information*, or for you to 'take care' of us. We've done just fine on our own."

"I know. I can see that," he said. "But you don't *have* to do it on your own. Not anymore. I want to help. I want to be there—for both of you. I want to be part of your lives."

"How? Your life isn't your own. You belong to your 'subjects,' to your family. To your *fiancée.* We're from totally different worlds. I have a child to protect. You've got a duty to uphold. You've got a country to serve. You've got Audrey. There's no place for AJ and me in that."

"That's not true. He's *my* son. He's heir to the principality of Aubernesse," Alex said.

"He's a four-year old boy," I practically shouted. "He doesn't know you at all. I won't let you take *my* son away from me, from all he's ever known and loved."

Alex blinked, apparently taken aback. His tone sounded wounded. "I would never do that. All I want is to be there for him—for both of you."

"You've just made that impossible. Goodbye Alex. Have a nice life. I hope you live happily ever after with your princess."

Alex's expression and tone hardened. "You can't possibly expect me to abandon my child now that I know about him. I won't do it, Cinda. Don't ask it of me."

"I'm not asking anything of you. I'm telling you—it's over." I resumed my slow trek to the SUV, frustrated by the injury that hindered me.

Alex followed me all the way to the parked vehicle.

"You think this is over?" he demanded in an incredulous tone. "Far from it. I will not spend the rest of my life being 'the pilot' to my child when I have the chance to be 'Daddy.'"

"*Had* the chance," I corrected as I yanked open the front passenger door and slid inside. "Don't follow me. *Don't* call me."

Slamming the door behind me, I dropped my face into my hands.

"I'm *so* sorry." Kristal's tone was grave. "I thought he knew. I thought you talked on the island. I never would have brought—"

"I know. Let's just go. Please," I muttered into my palms, not looking up until we'd pulled away.

Unable to resist checking the rearview mirror, I saw Alex still standing there in the middle of the parking lot, watching us go. His tall, powerful form sagged, making him look exhausted.

Defeated.

I shifted my tear-stained focus to the view out the windshield, shrugging off the light tapping of my conscience and trying feverishly to shut out the little voice that reminded me Alex hadn't been the *only* one who'd withheld important information.

It also asked a question... if he'd been defeated... did that mean I'd won? I certainly didn't feel victorious.

In fact, I felt a greater sense of loss than I'd ever experienced in my life—and that was saying a lot.

Turning to see my son's pout as he sulked in his booster seat in the rear of the SUV, my heart cracked, admitting fresh pain.

Because I knew who the real loser would be in this disastrous mess.

AJ.

TWENTY-FIVE

Two Options

Alex

Patton drove toward Oceanview Avenue while my head roared with anguish and my belly roiled with grief.

Obviously, I should have told Cinda about Audrey.

To me, it had been a non-issue. At some point before dawn, I'd made up my mind to speak with my family and tell them there would be no engagement announcement at tomorrow's ball. Then I'd speak to Audrey myself, explaining why I couldn't go through with the arranged marriage.

But Cinda didn't know all that. And now she didn't want to hear anything I had to say. I had no idea what to do. One thing was for sure—I wasn't leaving Eastport Bay until I'd straightened it all out.

A son. I have a son.

Fierce joy mixed with a sickening sense of fear in my chest. My son was here in this very city, within my reach. I could get to him in only a few minutes' drive time. And yet a life with AJ and Cinda seemed a million miles away right now.

As soon as the boy's dark eyes had met my identical ones,

I'd known he was mine. It was like looking at my own childhood photos.

And the look in Cinda's eyes when Patton had accidentally let my "secret" slip...*fuck*.

She hated me. And my son didn't know me at all. I had to fix it—somehow.

My mother accosted me as soon as I arrived at the mansion.

"Thank goodness you're home. Why would you have gone to the island with a storm coming?" she scolded. "You knew Audrey's family would be arriving, and it was foolish to fly in weather like that. It's not like you at all. At least the storm let up in time for the ball."

She stopped haranguing me for a second to look me over. "Oh dear, you look awful."

I gave her a droll look. "Thank you. I feel awful. I didn't sleep at all last night. Or the night before. Where is Dad?"

Mum blinked in apparent surprise at my surly attitude. "He's gone down to the harbor to tour the America's Cup racing boats with your brother. Why? What's wrong? What happened?"

"I'm not sure yet, but I *do* intend to find out. Please tell him I need to speak with him as soon as he returns. I'm going up to my suite now, and I don't want to be disturbed."

"But the deRamels..." she protested.

"Believe me, they *don't* want to meet me in my current state. I'll see you all at dinner." I walked away toward the staircase.

My mother no doubt thought I was referring to my disheveled appearance, but it was my state of mind I couldn't expose my potential future in-laws to. My head was a mess.

Back in Aubernesse, and even here in this house, my life was all about duty. It dropped on me like a heavy cloak the moment I stepped through the door.

Seeing Cinda had awakened the hope of a whole new life —a freer one, one full of joy and passion instead of just duty and honor.

I knew what my heart wanted, but it wasn't entirely up to me. If I couldn't get through to Cinda, if she didn't want me back... well, I would always know exactly what I was missing in life.

In that case, perhaps I *should* just go ahead with my father's plans. It was the path of least resistance and would make everyone else happy.

I'd never be happy—not truly—not without Cinda. I might end up married to someone else, but it would always be her I wanted.

How brutally unfair to Audrey. Didn't she deserve better than to spend her life with a man who loved another woman? I couldn't imagine anything more miserable.

Except perhaps *being* the man in love with that other woman.

There were really only two options—figure out a way to win Cinda back... or let her go forever. I had no idea how to accomplish either mission.

And I was too exhausted at the moment to think straight. Two consecutive nights of not sleeping and a surfeit of emotion had left me beyond muddled.

Once behind the closed doors of my suite, I went straight to my bed and fell onto it without bothering to pull back the coverlet. For several hours I slept hard. I didn't even dream as far as I was aware.

When I woke, there was one thought on my mind.

Rolling out of bed, I walked to the tall bureau where my valet had placed my folded clothing. I opened one of the smaller top drawers, reached inside, and withdrew the small velvet box I'd placed there nearly five years ago.

Opening it, I touched the twelve-carat sapphire that

reminded me so much of Cinda's deep blue eyes. The fourteen diamond solitaires that surrounded it were meant to remind her of the stars we'd gazed at from the beach at night.

A surge of despair weakened my knees as I remembered the pain of coming home on that long-ago night and tucking the ring back into its box instead of sliding it onto Cinda's left hand as I'd planned.

I hadn't had the heart to return it, but I also hadn't been able to stand seeing it. So I'd shoved it in the back of this drawer the same way I'd shoved all my feelings into a dark box deep inside my soul.

I'd flown home and told myself I was okay, that I could go on, get over it, that there would be someone else to take her place. Now I was acutely aware of just how much I'd been fooling myself.

The dark box? It was open now. Seeing Cinda had shined a spotlight on the feelings that had never dissipated but had only been hidden.

I made a decision. This ring *wouldn't* remain hidden.

It was just as perfect for Cinda now as it had been then. She might not want to marry me, but I'd give it to her anyway. She could wear it, flush it, or pawn it—it was up to her. But I *would* give it to her before I left Eastport Bay.

The idea revived me. Just the thought of seeing her again, even one more time, made life seem worth living.

And that was how I knew I couldn't go through with the marriage to Audrey—no matter how things went with Cinda.

Not bothering to change out of my wrinkled clothes, I left my suite, intending to find my almost-fiancée and speak with her honestly. My sister Jane was coming down the hall as I entered it.

"Well, if it isn't the daredevil pilot himself," she said in a jovial tone, tossing her fiery red hair and laughing. "I'm glad you didn't get blown away. We were all worried about you."

"No need. I'm perfectly all right."

"Yes, and how's Miss Last-Chance Fling?" she quipped.

"Who?"

"Cam and I were talking about it. We've been to the beach house there, remember? Hanging out on an oceanside cliff is the last place anyone would want to be with a hurricane approaching. You must have had one *hell* of a reason to be there. We both agreed it had to be a woman."

I shook my head, irritated. "I can't chat right now. I'm looking for Audrey. Do you know where she is?"

"As a matter of fact, I do. She's gone out to do a bit of 'retail therapy' with her sisters. She was *none* too pleased to arrive and find out you'd jetted away for a spur-of-the-moment trip. Planning to smooth things over with that famous Wessex charm, are we?" Janey teased.

"Cam is the one with all the charm. And I don't think there's enough charm in the world to cover this situation."

Her eyes widened with surprise and no small measure of glee.

"Why? What *have* you done Alex?"

"It's not what I've done," I informed her. "It's what I'm about to do. Fair warning—there may be a few *extra* fireworks at the ball tomorrow night."

TWENTY-SIX

I Still Do

Alex

That night, I stood at the front door of Cinda's small cottage, the ring in my pocket and a flicker of hope in my heart.

It was fighting not to be extinguished by the fear that she'd turn me away, that she'd refuse to even listen.

I had to try, though I still hadn't had a chance to speak with Audrey.

She hadn't come down to dinner this evening. In fact, she'd sent word she was spending the night with a friend instead of returning to the mansion after her shopping excursion.

Either she was trying to punish me for being absent when she'd arrived... or she *might* not be as upset about me breaking off our arrangement as I expected her to be.

Perhaps she had her own reasons for objecting to the political match. Either way, I couldn't wait any longer to straighten things out with Cinda.

Conscious of the late hour, I knocked softly instead of ringing the bell. There was the sound of movement on the other side of the door—no doubt Cinda was looking through the security port.

This was the moment of truth. Would she even open the door?

She did. But she didn't look happy about it.

"How did you find out where I live?" she asked, dropping her chin and sighing loudly through the cracked door.

I gave her a sheepish grin and held my hands out to the sides, palms up, offering a two-word answer. "Billionaire prince?"

Cinda smirked. "Yeah. I figured you'd use your 'royal resources' and show up here sooner or later. Well, I don't care how 'charming' you are... you weren't honest with me."

"You weren't completely honest with me, either, were you?"

Seeing the guilt in her expression, I sensed an opening and pounced on it. "In any case, I don't think the doorstep is the proper place to discuss it. May I come in? I'd like to talk."

Cinda hesitated a moment but nodded, opening the door further but stopping short of stepping back to allow me inside. She had on a baby pink nightshirt that fell to just above her knees and buttoned up the front. Her feet were bare.

"We can talk—about AJ," she said. "That's it. Nothing else is going to happen here tonight."

She seemed to be warning me away from trying to start a discussion about our relationship, and she was *definitely* making it clear sex was off the table.

But the door was open—I'd start there.

"Fine. Of course. I didn't expect anything more." The ring in my pocket said otherwise—but she didn't have to know about that. Yet.

Finally, Cinda stepped back and gestured for me to enter the house. Noticing the quiet, I looked around. "Is AJ in bed?"

She nodded. "He sleeps like a rock. Once he's down, he's out for the night."

I stepped into the small living room area. It was neat and casually furnished with a cheery yellow and red plaid couch against one wall and a worn-looking upright piano on the opposite wall. An upholstered wing back chair sat invitingly near the fireplace.

The white wood mantle was decorated with candles, a small bird's nest, and several vases of different heights that contained branches of colorful fall leaves. There were a lot of pillows and a couple of soft-looking throw blankets.

The place looked comfortable. It looked like... her. It looked like a *home*.

Framed photos adorned the side tables and shelves. All of them were of AJ. I was silent for several minutes as I walked around the room picking up the individual frames and studying the photos inside.

Each one pierced my heart with a tiny dart of longing and regret.

There was AJ's homecoming from the hospital, his first bath, and what appeared to be his first attempt at feeding himself. I laughed at that one, at the exuberant expression he wore while smearing food on his face and in his curly hair.

A powerful concoction of mixed emotions filled me. Guilt, shame, disbelief, and absolute wonderment at this little person who looked so much like me it was almost disorienting.

In many of the pictures Cinda was holding AJ, playing with him, cuddling and kissing him, so someone else must have been holding the camera. Someone other than me.

Jealousy wrapped around my vocal cords, making my voice come out in a strangled whisper. "He's so beautiful."

"He is," Cinda agreed. "He looks like you."

Something in her voice made me glance up to check her

expression. It was soft, her eyes glistening in the light from the fire.

"Can I see him?" I ventured. "I just want a peek."

She nodded and turned to walk down a short hallway. I followed, my pulse beginning to rush.

Cinda opened the first door on the right, and together we tiptoed into the room and stood at the side of AJ's molded plastic rocket ship bed. The nightlight revealed how he'd tossed in his sleep, throwing his blanket to the floor in the process. I bent over and picked it up, gently draping it over his tiny form.

Unable to help myself, I put a hand on the sleeping child's head, smoothing the silky, mussed hair away from his forehead. AJ stirred a bit but didn't wake, only clutched his stuffed airplane toy closer. A sharp, sweet pain pulsed in my chest.

My God—I love this kid already.

Cinda tapped me on the shoulder and jerked her head toward the door. I followed her out into the hallway and then the living room, clenching my fists to quell the trembling of my hands.

"I'm making tea. Want some?" she asked.

I was shaken enough to wish for something a bit stronger, but I said, "Sure. That would be nice."

"Have a seat in the living room. It'll just be a minute."

Cinda disappeared into the kitchen and returned five minutes later with a tray bearing two mugs, a tiny pitcher of cream, and a bowl with various sweetener choices.

She made a project of perfecting her teacup, stirring longer than necessary to blend its contents. I couldn't help but notice the trembling of her hands.

She seemed to be waiting for me to speak first, so I did.

"I'd like to apologize again for the way you found out about Audrey. It wasn't my intention to keep it a secret. I was planning to tell you. I just needed some time to sort things out."

Cinda's response came out in a rush. "I'm sorry too for the way I spoke to you today. I was in shock. And I hope you know I wasn't hiding AJ from you—well, not until a few days ago. When I found out I was pregnant, I didn't know how to reach you. I had no way of finding you. When I saw you again this week... I was afraid of how you'd react."

When I didn't immediately respond—I was trying to find the right words—her defensiveness converted to indignation.

"Do you think I *wanted* to raise a child on my own? Wanted to endure the dirty looks and the judgment, wanted to suffer through all the long, sleepless nights, the terrible twos, not to mention twenty-six hours of labor, alone?"

I reached up to take her flushed cheeks between my palms. "I'm not angry with *you*. I'm angry with my family for forcing me to leave the country before I'd found you—with myself for letting them. I *knew* you wouldn't just abandon me without a goodbye. I knew what we had was real, and I talked myself out of it because my feelings were hurt."

Dropping my hands, I added, "I do wish you'd told me about AJ on the island. It was quite a shock to the system to see a vision of my own childhood self trotting across the parking lot."

"I should have. I almost did, but I chickened out. I guess we've both made mistakes," she said softly.

"Yeah." I sat back, first staring up at the ceiling then collapsing into the couch cushions and dragging a hand through my hair.

This was it. My chance to make things right, to convince Cinda there was a future for us as a family. I turned my head to look over at her.

"I can't believe... all this time... I had no idea he even existed. I had no idea what you were going through. I'm *so sorry* I wasn't there when you needed me. It must have been awful going through childbirth alone. I should have been there holding your hand, feeding you ice chips or whatever it is they give fathers to do so they don't feel utterly useless during the process."

Cinda's expression crumpled, her eyes reddening. I was getting through to her—at least I hoped so.

"You had to raise an infant with no help—*while* working to put food on the table," I said. "Meanwhile I've been traipsing around the globe attending parties where the catering expense alone probably would have paid your bills for a year."

"It's not your fault, Alex," she said. "You didn't know."

My fingertips dug into my jeans. My voice sounded like gravel. "But I *should* have. I should never have stopped until I found you. I wish I had been there to hold him, to take some of those night shifts early on."

"I nursed him, so I would have had to get up anyway."

"Yes, but I could have brought him to you, so you didn't have to get out of bed. He could have slept there between us where I could have watched him dream. And now he's *four*—I've missed everything."

The mental picture seemed to resonate with her. She reached out and covered my hand with her small, cool one.

"Not everything. He's only four. There's a lot of his childhood left. Plenty of dreams still to come." She paused. "I'm sure he'd love to have a father to share them with."

My heart sprang to attention. "You think so?"

She nodded. "I know so. He's old enough now that he realizes most of his friends have fathers who live with them. He's started asking me where *his* daddy is."

I felt like I'd been punched. "What do you tell him?"

"I told him his daddy loves him but has to live far away, that maybe he'd meet him someday." She shrugged. "It was the best I could come up with. He's too young right now to understand the truth."

"That *is* the truth—part of it anyway. I do love him. It doesn't make any sense because we just met today, but I feel like I already love him because I loved you so much."

After a beat, I pushed a long overdue confession past the lump crowding my throat. "I still do."

Cinda's intake of breath was audible. She looked away toward the fire and withdrew her hand, placing it at the base of her throat where she fiddled with her shirt collar.

"It was all a long time ago. We've moved on, and—"

"I didn't. Not really." I grabbed her hand again and squeezed.

The ring in my pocket seemed to take on weight and pulse, eager for the moment I'd pull it out and slide it onto her finger where it belonged.

"I never got over you," I confessed. "Even when I thought you didn't want me anymore, I still longed for you. I told myself it was stupid to still want you, but I couldn't help it. And then when I saw you again last week... you took my breath away. I was right back in love, as if not a day had passed since our last kiss."

"Alex," she whispered. She looked like she was fighting tears.

"I want to make up for lost time—with AJ and with you. I want us to be together, the three of us. Do you have passports? If not, I know someone who can expedite them for you."

I rattled off plans a mile a minute, my voice—and my heart—filled with excitement and certainty.

That was when I noticed Cinda didn't look so certain.

And she hadn't said she loved me back.

TWENTY-SEVEN
Impossible Dream

Cinda

"Alex, wait. Stop. Listen to me."

He stopped talking and watched me intently. I took a deep breath and let it out, gathering my thoughts. I had to say this right.

I had to make things clear to him if there was ever to be any hope of us co-parenting AJ successfully.

After I'd recovered from the unplanned airport reunion scene and calmed down, I'd spent the day thinking about it and kept coming back to the same conclusion—AJ's life *would* be better with Alex in it.

But we'd never be a real family. Alex could be a sort of... enhancement to AJ's life, an occasional visitor, and perhaps someday when AJ was grown, even a friend and mentor.

But a visitation arrangement for our son would be as far as things could go between Alex and me. In spite of my behavior yesterday on the island, I had no interest in being a "royal consort" or whatever fancy name the citizens of Aubernesse would label our relationship.

That interlude between us, as romantic and erotic as it had been, would be the last.

"The thing is," I said, "time has passed. We're not the kids we were back then. We've changed. Both of us."

Alex's forehead wrinkled in confusion. "Do you not feel the same then? I thought maybe... after what happened between us yesterday..."

"I got... carried away. That shouldn't have happened. It's *not* going to happen again. Anyway, *feelings* are not the issue. But there are lots of others." I extracted my hand from his once more and rose to pace the room.

"Think about it. You live in a different country. You're a royal. I'm just a regular girl from Eastport Bay. I was a maid when you met me, for God's sake. Remember how you used to tell me we couldn't act like a couple when your parents were at the beach club? Now I understand why—and I get it. They're not going to approve of me any more now than they would have back then. *Less*, probably. I'm a commoner, a single mom. Besides, I have a company to run here in Eastport Bay. I have friends here and family depending on me."

He smiled. "All of that can be worked out. My family will get over it—in time. Perhaps they'll even be thrilled. My mother's always on my back about producing a royal heir. As it turns out I've already got one—AJ. And as far as your work, I have more money than anyone could spend in several lifetimes. I'll take care of you. I'll take care of my son. Did you think I would just shirk my obligations?"

At the suggestion that I place my son's future and my own security in his hands, I balked. "We're not 'obligations.' We're people. People who have lives and minds of our own."

Alex backtracked immediately, coming off the couch in a swift move and approaching me.

"I know that. That came out all wrong. I'm just excited. I feel like a starving man who's just been dropped into a warehouse full of food. I can tell you don't like the idea of relying on someone. I can't blame you. And I won't pressure you."

He came closer, and I backed away, afraid of what would happen if I allowed him to touch me. He didn't, but he followed me, slowly stalking until the backs of my thighs met the old piano on the wall behind me.

"We can go slow, take as long as you like to acclimate to the idea." His voice was gentle, reasonable. It was also deep and husky and unbelievably sexy—which made it hard to concentrate on the reasonable part.

"We'll get to know each other again," he said. "I can stay here in Eastport Bay and spend some time with AJ so we can get to know each other as well. Whatever you want."

I relaxed a bit, understanding Alex wouldn't be forcing his will on us. And I realized it couldn't have been easy on him, learning he'd missed out on four years of his child's life and then being told he'd have to wait.

My heart softened, along with my tone.

"I do want you to get to know AJ. He's the most wonderful little boy. But this is going to be a big shock for him. We'll have to think of a way to tell him that won't freak him out. He's used to it being just the two of us. It's all he's ever known."

Now Alex did touch me, resting his big hands on my shoulders. Just that small amount of contact sparked the helpless attraction I felt for him into flame.

Raw need vibrated through my body at his nearness. I was a *mess* when it came to this man.

"Thank you," he murmured.

"For what?"

"For the chance. And for taking such good care of our little boy. I'll never forgive myself for giving up too easily, for not being there."

I was quiet for a moment, just staring up at him, at the

sincerity and regret in his eyes. The other emotions in them I didn't really want to think about at the moment.

Because he looked like he needed and wanted me just as desperately as I craved him.

"AJ will forgive you," I said finally in a last, desperate attempt to steer the conversation into safe territory.

His eyes shined with hope. "Do you really think so?"

"I do."

There was a long pause. Alex swallowed, hesitated, finally spoke. "Can you forgive me?"

I nodded, swallowing back tears. "I already have."

Cradling my face with one hand, he wiped away an escaped drop of moisture with his thumb, and my breath left me.

Accompanied by all my sense, apparently.

I hadn't intended to let this happen tonight, to allow any sort of intimacy. I'd wanted to keep it all business—two parents working out a visitation schedule that would be beneficial to their son.

But the yearning look in Alex's eyes paralyzed me, drawing me toward the flame like an enthralled moth destined for a fiery end.

His head lowered, and I didn't move away. Did nothing to stop him. His lips descended to mine, joining them in a kiss that was at first light and gentle, almost worshipful.

Then in a flash of heat and hunger it changed.

The swell of emotion nearly knocked me off my feet. Once again, I was a twenty-four-year-old, falling in love for the first time.

Alex's kiss took me right back to those days at the beach, those nights under the stars when I'd thought I might die from the acute pleasure of his kiss and touch.

Now, just like then, I couldn't seem to get enough of him, couldn't get close enough. My fingers sank into the heavy layers of his hair then coasted over his broad shoulders and firm chest, down to his hard abdomen and sides.

My hips canted forward, cradling the hardness that grew between us and pressed against my belly. Feeling the evidence of his desire for me, the place between my legs went wet.

Nothing was a bigger turn on than knowing how hard I made him. I gave into the craving and allowed my hand to slip between us, coasting my palm over the enticing bulge.

Alex's breathing sped up and became audible. While he'd been making an obvious effort to keep a respectful distance before, he responded to my unmistakable signs, letting his hands move over me, returning touch for touch.

One of his hands caressed my breast while the other dragged my nightshirt up my thighs. His fingers searched between my legs. When he felt the dampness of my panties, he broke the kiss and gasped, and his lungs started working harder.

"You are so fucking sexy," he panted against my lips. "I can't keep my hands off you."

"Apparently I can't keep my hands off you either—although I should." Mine went to the front of his jeans, shaking, fumbling with his zipper in my hurry to get it open.

Alex decided to help me, quickly unbuttoning them and ripping the zipper down. I slid my hand inside and gripped him greedily, earning a pleasured groan. He felt huge and hot and oh so ready.

Touching him like this was the fulfillment of all the fantasies I'd tried but failed to keep at bay the past few years.

God, how I want this man. I wanted him over me, inside me, all around me. I wanted to be owned, occupied, and taken by him.

Just once more. One more time.

His breaths hit my neck in steamy puffs as he kissed me there. Dragging the collar of my sleepshirt to the side, he kissed his way down to my collarbone before undoing the buttons and pushing the garment open to reveal my bare breasts.

The tips of them contracted in the cool air but he covered them, one with a warm, slowly circling palm and the other with his mouth.

I gasped and writhed at the lush glide of his tongue, the wet heat sending pleasure thumping through my body.

It had been a long time since I'd felt weak in the knees, but my wobbly legs would no longer support me. I leaned heavily against the piano, half sitting on its closed lid as my hips rocked forward in a blind, rhythmic quest for contact with his body—any part of it, as long as he would touch me.

Attentive to every movement and sound I made, Alex reached to soothe the area that was so swollen and aching for him.

His fingers burrowed beneath the elastic band of my panties, seeking and finding the soft layers of sensitive flesh, caressing me in ever-shrinking circles until he reached a place of exquisite pulsing pleasure.

His tongue slid across mine in long, lewd kisses while he touched me the way only he ever had. I was ravenous for him, intimate muscles clenching on an emptiness I was desperate for him to fill.

Just thinking of that thick length plunging into me, taking possession of my body, sent my thoughts whirling and sparks sizzling to my core.

The glowing heat boiled over in a meltdown of madness and pleasure, and I hunched and shuddered as my nails dug into his biceps, coming hard on his hand.

The final jolt rocked the garage sale piano, causing the instrument to vibrate with a low, discordant sound.

When I opened my eyes, Alex was wearing a wide, satisfied grin. "I do believe that's my best work on the piano to date."

I couldn't do much more than whimper in response, which was fine since Alex didn't seem to need one.

"I want to taste you again," he said in a low, sensuous growl. "I haven't been able to think about anything else since yesterday on that couch after the storm."

He reached under my sleepshirt and dragged my panties downward. When they dropped to the floor, he followed, kneeling in front of me.

But I stopped him with a hand to his chest. "Uh uh. My turn to play."

TWENTY-EIGHT

Right Back to Where We Left Off

Cinda

One of Alex's dark eyebrows lifted.

He looked amused and completely turned on, laughing as I backed him across the room to the couch and pushed him to the cushions with a gentle shove.

He landed with a soft bounce, smiling up at me, his brown eyes smoldering. "Well, if you insist."

"I do."

My mouth watering, I gripped the top of his jeans and boxer briefs and yanked them down together. When they got to his knees, Alex kicked them off the rest of the way, requiring me to move back a little.

I took advantage of the moment to appreciate the picture in front of me. Sprawled there on my ten-year-old plaid couch, amidst the feminine throw pillows and blankets, Alex looked enormous.

He also looked unbearably sexy with all that bronze skin stretched tight over sleek muscle. I dropped to my knees in front of him, pushing his spread legs wider.

Alex's gorgeous lips fell apart, and his eyes blazed with

black fire. "My God, Cinda. You have no idea how many times I dreamed of this moment."

His eyes squeezed shut when I wrapped my hand around his erection, and I think my groan was even louder than his. He felt so, so good, the smooth skin feverish and pulsing with its own heartbeat.

He pushed forward, driving himself into my hand, and I stroked the hard length, gratified to feel it growing even harder.

When I dipped my head and took him into my mouth... well it was a good thing AJ slept like a log. Alex's moan was loud and long and probably the most erotic sound I'd ever heard in my life.

Encouraged, I swirled my tongue over the throbbing tip and down the shaft, trying to taste as much of him as possible.

Within a matter of seconds, I was plucked from between his legs and hauled up onto his lap, straddling him face to face.

"You're much too good at that," he wheezed, sounding like he'd just sprinted for ten miles. Uphill.

"Like riding a bike, I guess. I haven't done it since that summer five years ago."

For a second, he went stock still beneath me. His arrested gaze swept over my face, searching for deception.

"You haven't..." He seemed to be casting about for a polite way to say it.

Failing to find one, he asked flat out, "You haven't gone down on anyone else? Ever?"

I shook my head, pressing a kiss to his jaw just below his ear, where I remembered the skin being extra sensitive. I remembered *everything* about the times we'd been together—including how much he'd loved it when I'd gotten on my knees for him.

So why had he stopped me this time?

"I haven't done *anything* with anyone else. Only you," I told him.

He shook his head in apparent wonder. He also looked immensely pleased. "I was your first... and I'll be your last."

I started to interrupt. "We don't know that. We don't know if—"

But Alex cut me off, curling his hands around my head and covering my mouth with burning kisses that stole my breath. As our tongues tangled, his hands left my hair to slide down my shoulders then around to the front where they pushed inside the listing sides of my sleepshirt to my naked skin.

He gently shaped my waist then my ribcage then cupped my breasts, thumbing the tips of them until the nipples were peaked and aching. Then he palmed my bottom, pulling me as tightly as possible against his hard-on.

I rocked forward, shamelessly rubbing myself against the base of it before rising on my knees so I could sink down on him.

Alex's grip on my hips stopped me mid-motion.

"Wait. Wait," he gasped.

Leaning his forehead against my chest, he breathed in heavy gusts. "I don't have any condoms. Again."

He let out a frustrated growl. "I came over here to talk to you—I didn't think there was any possibility of anything like this happening. You don't happen to be on the pill, do you?"

Sliding my hands over the inviting dark scruff on his jaw, I lifted his face so our eyes met.

"I am actually—but not for the usual reason. As I told you, I have no sex life. *Had* no sex life," I corrected with a little laugh. "I seem to be having one now, suddenly."

His fingers sank deeper into my hips, belying his tenuous hold on self-control. "So then, how would you feel about... I mean, are you okay with..."

My laugh was louder now. "Apparently so since I was about to ride you bareback like an Andalusian stallion. Hopefully a stallion who hasn't been sowing his royal oats all over the world?"

A question I probably should have asked a little sooner.

He didn't laugh at my joke. "If you're asking whether I sleep around, the answer is no. I can't say there's been *no one* since you—I tried to drown my sorrows for a while after I lost you, in whatever intoxicating substances I could find. But that ended a long time ago. I haven't been with anyone in well over a year, and the royal physicians are *very* thorough in their examinations. I'm clean."

We stared at each other for a long moment then, as if by unspoken agreement, our mouths crashed together, and our bodies went right back to where we left off.

Levering myself upward, I sank down onto Alex in a supple slide that sent whorls of sensation from my core to the tips of every extremity. He felt incredible inside me, solid, heavy, enduring.

Something about the steadfast feeling of having him buried deep inside me brought tears to my eyes.

I felt... unlocked, like a combination safe that had been a digit short of opening for the past few years and now stood with the door swung ajar.

Everything I'd been keeping safely sealed away was now out in the open, vulnerable.

Alex must have been affected too, because his breath came out in a whoosh, and his eyes squeezed tightly shut for a second before they opened to connect with mine.

"We fit together perfectly," he murmured, beginning to move inside me. "We were meant to be together. Can't you feel it?"

At that moment, I would have answered pretty much any question in the affirmative.

Do you like pickles dipped in peanut butter and fire ants? Yes.

Want to ride a rollercoaster with a five-hundred foot drop and no safety bars? Sure, why not?

We were meant to be together—can't you feel it? YES *Yes yes yes.*

I didn't realize some of those Yes's had actually come out of my mouth until I saw Alex's exuberant smile.

It wasn't true of course. We weren't a perfect fit—outside of the bedroom anyway. Speaking of…

"We should go to my room." I glanced over my shoulder to the empty hallway. "Just in case. He's a sound sleeper, but you never know."

Without a word, Alex rose from the couch, our bodies still locked together. He urged me to wrap my arms and legs around him as he carried me down the short hallway to the door I indicated.

Depositing me on the bed, he went back and locked the door, then returned to me, climbing over me and spreading my legs wide.

I didn't argue. I was up for anything and everything—for one night only.

This was my last chance to show him everything he'd meant to me, would always mean to me, and take from him everything I'd ever get to have.

Alex eased inside me again, and the two of us began a sensory slide, touching, gripping, tasting.

He murmured endearments steadily, words of sex and love and wicked plans, all the while impaling me with regular, disciplined thrusts.

I clung to his strong back, gnawing at the side of his neck, licking at his hot skin and the beads of sweat that rose on its surface. I loved everything about this man, the way he moved, the way he smelled and looked, and the maddeningly sexy sounds he made when I touched him and drove him crazy.

I lifted my hips against his, and the rhythm of his strokes picked up pace. One of them hit me just right, pressing the front of my body in a way that sent waves of pleasure through me and made me cry out.

"Yes," he whispered. "Come for me again Cinda. Come, sweet girl."

Though I wasn't as loud as I'd been at the beach house, it was hard to suppress the groans of pleasure as Alex repeated the movement, grinding into me again and again at the perfect angle.

One thrust pushed me past the tipping point, and I bucked upward and stifled a scream, managing to lift Alex a few inches before he drove downward again.

Catching and drinking in the pleasure sounds with his mouth, he pinned me to the bed and milked a few more voluptuous spasms of pleasure from my already pleasure-drunk body before he shoved himself deep and shuddered.

After a moment of stillness, he rolled off of me to his side, pulling me with him and tucking me into the crook of his shoulder with my head on his chest.

Though his body was entirely relaxed, Alex didn't seem sleepy at all. His lips browsed over my forehead and cheekbones while his hands wandered everywhere, petting, massaging, squeezing and stroking.

I felt exhausted and more satisfied than I'd ever been in my life. And sad.

I clung to him, wanting the moment to never end.

But it had to. Being with him like this had made me feel impossibly young again, but I was *not* a girl anymore. I was a responsible adult who could control her decisions and actions and emotions.

Mostly.

Who could be wise instead of reckless. Who could put common sense above desire… even when it hurt.

And it was about to.

Alex rested his chin atop my head, stroking my hair and back as he held me tightly against him. His voice was a deep rumble under my cheek.

"I know you said nothing was going to happen tonight, but it's too easy to lose control with you—I've wanted you for too long." His tone was of the sorry-not-sorry variety.

I nodded, relishing the feel of his hot skin against my face and the textures of his uber-masculine body under my fingertips.

"It's okay. I wanted it, too… clearly."

Alex lifted his head and shifted back a bit so he could see my face. His was nothing short of jubilant.

His eyes flared, and his gaze dropped to my lips. He dipped his head, moving in to kiss me and start it all over again—which I had no doubt he was capable of doing.

I pulled back, squirming to extricate myself from his hold.

This was it. I had to say it—now, before he *did* get me going and I forgot how to speak.

Sitting up and tucking the top sheet around myself, I made my tone firm, businesslike.

"But that was the last time."

TWENTY-NINE

Naked Honesty

Cinda

There. I'd said it, and I sounded almost convincing enough to believe it myself.

Alex's face went blank. "What?"

"We can't keep doing this. As… nice as it is… kissing you—and all the rest—co-parenting is all there can be between us going forward."

His brows lowered and drew together, and his mouth hardened. "That's ridiculous. What about what just happened? That was the best sex of my life—hands down. As far as I could tell, you enjoyed it, too."

"I did. And I wanted to do that with you—this once—for old times' sake. But we can't keep doing it."

"I'd love to know why not."

"You *do* know. I mean… it can't *lead* to anything, so it's only going to hurt more in the long run. At least it'll hurt me."

His expression was stormy, and his tone was bruised. "Have you not heard a word I said all night? We fit together. We *belong* together. I love you, Cinda. I want you in my life, and by that, I mean every day. Not as a *co-parent*. As my wife. I think the past half hour proves you want me, too."

Alex waited for my response, wearing a look that suggested he doubted my comprehension skills—or maybe my sanity.

My heart ached like a migraine in my chest. On the outside, I remained impassive. "It'll never work."

"Why not?" Alex's baffled expression morphed into something more vulnerable. "Unless... *you* don't love *me*?"

I could lie. He might even believe me.

But this was a moment for naked honesty. We'd have to deal with each other for the rest of our lives—for AJ's sake. We couldn't be together as a couple, but at the very least I wanted us to be truthful with each other.

"No. I do."

Swallowing hard, I looked down before meeting his eyes again. "I do love you, Alex. I never stopped. But contrary to what the fairy tales tell you, love doesn't conquer all. Your family—your country—will never accept me as your wife. They'll never acknowledge AJ as anything more than a bastard. The son of a cleaning lady."

The look on Alex's face told me he knew I was right.

And this was why I *couldn't* depend on him—he wasn't living in reality but a fantasy world that would shatter as soon as it was put under pressure. I had to stick with what I could count on—my business, my friends here in Eastport Bay.

Myself.

Alex was silent for a moment, breathing in and out several times. When he spoke again, his voice was filled with determination.

"I'll walk away. From all of it. I was willing to do it five years ago. I'm doubly willing now."

I shook my head, tears filling my eyes and the lump in my throat making it hard to speak. "That's a pipe dream. You can't just walk away from your home, from your family, your country, everything you know. Even if you were willing to actually do it, I couldn't let you. I know how painful it is to lose the people you love. I don't want that for you. I don't want AJ to go through that pain either."

Alex tensed. "What are you saying? You've changed your mind about allowing me to see him?"

"No. I won't stop you from seeing AJ, but the fact is you live in Aubernesse, and we live here. You have to go home sooner or later. I don't want AJ to... to come to rely on you... to love you... when you can't really be there for him."

"You're asking me not to tell him I'm his father."

I had to compose myself before continuing.

"I'm asking you to protect him—his little heart. Think carefully before you make promises to him you can't keep, before you say and do things that will make him love you and then turn around and leave him."

Alex's eyelids narrowed in an assessing gaze. "I see what's going on here. Is it AJ's heart you're trying to protect? Or is it *you* who's afraid to rely on someone and risk *your* heart?"

I ignored his astute question. "You can have visitation with AJ—*here*—in Rhode Island. I'll make sure the days and times are reasonable and generous. Just... have your assistant or whoever contact me, and we'll set up some kind of arrangement."

"No," Alex said. His face was a contorted mask of pain and frustration.

He gripped my shoulders, the pressure firm but not bruising. "I don't want an *arrangement.* I want a *family*—with you, with our son."

The words ripped my heart out. How I'd longed for us to be a family. When AJ was a newborn, I'd dreamed of Alex sweeping back into my life and telling me he missed me, that he wanted us both.

But that was then—before I knew the whole truth about him.

Before I realized how impossible that dream really was.

"The only true family I've ever had was my father," I said. "He was someone I could count on, someone I could trust completely. Can you honestly tell me you'll be that kind of father?"

"Yes. I can. I will. I want you and AJ more than I ever wanted any of that other stuff. Don't shut me out, Cinda, please."

Alex sounded so sincere I knew he believed what he was saying. But he had no idea what it was like to be a parent, or what it was like to have everyone you'd ever loved and counted on ripped away from you.

"That's what you say now," I told him. "You're speaking from emotion and not experience. You've never lived without all that 'stuff.' You don't know what it's like to struggle and live in the real world. But we've been here before, you and I. The fact is there's no place for me in your world. There never was. And there's no place for you in mine. I don't need you in it. I don't... want you."

The lie almost choked me, but I went on, sliding out of bed and backing toward the bathroom where I planned to hide and, if possible, drown in the shower.

"Please. Just... go home, Alex. If you really love me, you'll respect my wishes. Go home. Do your duty. Live your life."

I swallowed hard. "And marry Audrey."

THIRTY

The Helpers

Cinda

Thank God it was Saturday.

For one thing, AJ didn't have school, and I'd been able to spend the day with him. I'd missed him so much while I was away on the island it had been physically painful.

For another, I just didn't think I could handle going into the office. I'd slept fitfully, awakened again and again by sweetly tormenting dreams of Alex.

It didn't help that my sheets smelled like him.

Finally at about four a.m. I'd gotten up, ripped them off the bed, and started a load of laundry.

Though my mind was convinced I'd done the right thing sending him away, my body wasn't so sure.

It was firmly on the side of Team-Do-Whatever-We-Have-To-Do-To-Keep-Sleeping-With-the-Crown-Prince-of-Multiple-Orgasms.

Now it was early evening, and I was still in my pajamas, or more specifically the t-shirt and sweatpants that had served as last night's sleepwear. It had been a spectacularly unproductive day.

I'd gotten nothing done beyond puttering, though my bathrooms needed cleaning, and I needed to pay bills, catch up on missed emails, rake the leaves overflowing the yard, and shop for groceries.

It was just hard to do anything with that hole in my chest. What I'd told Alex had been true—I'd been fine before he arrived—at least I'd thought I was fine.

But now? Now I was acutely aware of something missing from my life. Alex's sudden, stunning presence had left me fully cognizant of his current absence.

Of the fact I would never stop missing him for the rest of my life.

Alex had texted early this morning. The message had torn my heart in half:

I will always be here, waiting for you to change your mind, ready to help, ready to love you and our son.

I would have to change my number because I wasn't going to make it if he kept contacting me and saying things like that.

Knowing him though, those sorts of messages would stop once he was married—he'd be faithful to his new wife.

The thought drained my remaining energy. There would be no cleaning, raking, or shopping today.

Wandering to the counter, I picked up a pile of mail and carried it to the kitchen table where my son was busily drawing.

AJ had asked about Alex, but not knowing what the possible visitation schedule might look like, I'd simply told him pilots couldn't stay in one place for long, they had to fly away again, and that he'd probably see Alex sometime soon.

I still wasn't sure how to tell him he'd met his father yesterday in that airport parking lot.

"Look at my picture, Mommy," AJ said.

Distracted, I glanced up and gave the colorful drawing a

cursory glance. "That's nice, honey. Who are all those people?"

"These are the helpers." AJ slid the paper toward me so I could more clearly see the firefighter, police officer, and doctor he'd drawn. There were two other figures on the page. AJ's ever-present prince. And a pilot.

My heart ripped further, the shreds of it hanging limply inside my chest.

"Miss Angelina has been teaching us about finding the helpers and the good people," AJ said.

I couldn't stop a cynical thought from popping out. "Sometimes it's hard to tell who's who."

The remark had been made under my breath, but apparently AJ's four-year-old super-hearing picked it up.

He responded with a chipper, "It's easy. Miss Angelina says you know them by what they do. Like you—you help people by cleaning their houses, and you give other people jobs to clean houses. And you help me."

He gave me the grin that never failed to melt my heart. A heart that was feeling pretty battered today, but I managed a smile in return.

Standing, I kissed the top of his head and walked a few steps away to start preparing his dinner. I had just enough energy to put together a peanut butter sandwich and some mixed fruit.

Thankfully, AJ wouldn't complain—he'd eat PB and J any time of day or night.

"Does anybody help *you*, Mommy?"

The innocent question stopped me in my tracks. Shaking it off and moving toward the pantry again, I took out a loaf of bread and carried it to the counter.

"I don't need anyone to help me," I told him carefully. "Mommy can do everything all by herself."

AJ's little face creased with a disapproving frown. "Miss

Angelina says we all need other people, and it's okay to let someone help you. Because that's what life is all about, living together, and working together, and helping each other."

I froze in the midst of applying peanut butter to a slice of bread, the knife stopping mid-air. A blob of peanut butter dropped and squelched on the countertop with a soft plunk.

That was when the tears started.

They overflowed my eyelids and rolled down my face, accompanied by hitching sobs I was powerless to control.

AJ lifted his head and looked at me in alarm. "Are you okay, Mommy?"

Unable to answer and trying desperately to control myself, I nodded. It was like a dam had broken inside me. The tears and sobs flowed, uncontrolled. I was suddenly, without warning, at the end of my own strength.

I *didn't* want to do it all alone.

AJ's teacher was right. Relying on people was part of life. Perhaps you *could* technically make it through life all on your own—I'd been proving it these past few years—but it felt more like survival than living.

Emotionally I was just as stranded and isolated as Alex and I had been on that island in the midst of a hurricane.

While trying to protect AJ and myself from the "storm," I'd cut myself off from other people, from my own feelings.

And I was hurting my son in the process. I wasn't modeling a healthy, connected life. Worse, I was depriving him of a father who wanted to know him, support him, and be there for him full time.

A small hand patted my leg as AJ, who was no doubt baffled and probably frightened by my sudden crying jag, tried to comfort me.

"It's okay, Mommy. I'll help you. I'm a good helper."

Sinking to the floor, I drew him onto my lap, hugging him close and rocking. "You sure are, buddy. You're the best."

AJ pulled his head away from my chest and patted my cheeks between his little palms. "Are you better now?"

I nodded, smiling through a few leftover tears. "I'm getting better, thanks to you. But there's something I need to do. Want to go over to Kristal's house for a visit with me?"

He jumped up, raising one extended arm over his head like a superhero. "Yes!"

"Okay, good. Go get your shoes on. I'll grab my purse, and we can head right over."

Alex had said he was returning to Aubernesse tomorrow, which meant I needed to speak with him *tonight*.

Panic struck with an invigorating, icy blast as I realized what else was happening tonight—the ball—the announcement of Alex's engagement.

The engagement I'd told him *not* to cancel.

I had leaned on my best friend too much this week already, but I texted Kristal, asking if it was okay to stop by and drop AJ off for a short while.

Cinda: I wouldn't ask if it wasn't an emergency. I'll explain when I get there.

Kristal: Of course. Come on over.

Within ten minutes AJ and I were in my old Civic and headed for the Bellevue Avenue mansion Kristal and Hunter shared.

"Wow, Mommy, look at all those big black cars," AJ said, pressing his nose to the backseat window.

"Those are limousines," I told him. "People rent them for special occasions."

"I want to be a lemma-zeen driver when I grow up."

"Sounds like fun. I bet you'll be a great driver."

While thrilling for my four-year-old to witness, the parade of slow-moving limos was actually a bit annoying to me. Now that I'd decided on a course of action, I didn't want to wait.

Finally, we made it to Kristal's house, ringing the bell at the back door.

Within seconds, Kristal opened it, smiling. "Hi. Come in, come in."

She bent down to do a special handshake with AJ. The two of them had developed it a few weeks ago, and he'd been making me practice it with him at home. When they'd flawlessly completed all the steps, he and Kristal high-fived, and AJ laughed.

"We did it!"

"That was awesome," Kristal said. "Hey, AJ, guess what? The cook just took a batch of brownies out of the oven. Want to go into the kitchen and ask her for one?"

He turned to me with wide, eager eyes.

I nodded, feeling guilty. "Go ahead. And be sure to say thank you." To Kristal I said, "I haven't even given him dinner yet. I'm not doing my best adulting today."

Once AJ had sped away as fast as his short legs could carry him, Kristal and I went into the cozy den to talk. "Okay now, tell me what's going on. What's the emergency? Does this have anything to do with Alex?"

"Why do you look so hopeful?" I asked.

"Well, he *may* have called and texted me begging for help —don't ask how he got my number because I have no idea. He really loves you, Cin."

"He *did*. But I blew it. He's going to marry someone else."

"I don't think so," Kristal said. "Not if you give him the slightest shred of hope."

Shaking my head, I also shook of my friend's matchmaking optimism. "I said some pretty cold things last night when I was upset."

"So I heard. He was definitely heartsick, but he wouldn't have been calling me if he'd given up completely."

"You don't think it's too late?" I asked.

Kristal checked the clock on the mantle. "Not yet... but the ball's started already."

"Oh my gosh. I've got to go." I popped off the couch and gave Kristal a quick hug. "Thanks so much for watching AJ. I won't be gone long."

I turned and started to leave, but Kristal snagged the back of my shirt. Her voice was filled with amusement. "Wait a minute. You're not planning to go over there like *that,* are you?"

Oh. I looked down at myself. Ratty sweatpants, sneakers, and a t-shirt that sported a peanut butter smudge I hadn't been aware of until this moment.

"Right. Not exactly glamorous." Then I shrugged. "It's not important. I'll ask him to come out and talk to me in the driveway or something. I don't want to take the chance of running into his fiancée anyway."

Kristal laughed. "Oh no. I don't think so. I'm not letting my best friend go to a royal ball to win back her prince looking like she's been hanging out with Oscar the Grouch in real life."

Placing a hand on each of my shoulders, Kristal steered me farther into the mansion, toward the staircase leading up to the upstairs bedroom suites.

"Where are we going?" I asked.

"To my room. You're going to let *me* play Fairy Godmother for a change and dress you up. I have tons of formal dresses. I'm sure one will fit you. And you know how good I am at hair and makeup."

She giggled with excitement. "You, my friend, are going to look like a princess tonight."

THIRTY-ONE

Not Royal Material

Cinda

Kristal and AJ dropped me off in front of the Wessex mansion forty minutes later.

"You look pretty, Mommy," he said with a shy smile as I got out and stood beside the car in the drive.

"Thank you, baby."

I had to admit, Kristal had done an amazing job transforming me from workaholic middle-class mom to glamorous high-society party guest.

The dress she'd loaned me (and pinned me into) was a dreamy confection of embroidered midnight blue tulle, sprinkled with Swarovski crystals.

She'd added tiny, sparkling crystals to my updo to match. The makeup Kristal had applied was subtle, making me look not "made up" but like I'd had a week's worth of great sleep and fresh air.

"All thanks to Kristal's magic wand," I told AJ with a wink.

His head whipped around to look at Kristal, and he

opened his mouth wide, clearly impressed. "You have a magic wand?"

Kristal and I both laughed, and Kristal leaned over to the passenger side window, waving something. "Don't forget this —your invitation."

"You mean *your* invitation." I took the crisp, white embossed card. "Hopefully I can pass for a Bellevue Avenue aristocrat—at least for a few minutes."

"You'll do better than pass. You look like you were born to it."

I rolled my eyes at Kristal's compliment and waved goodbye to AJ as he beamed at me from the back seat. Holding up the hem of my dress, I walked up the drive to the mansion's enormous front door.

Despite my fears of being turned away, the butler who opened it barely gave the invitation a glance.

He extended his arm in an inviting gesture. "Welcome madam. Enjoy the party."

Nerves firing and popping all over my body, I followed the sounds of orchestra music and crowd chatter through the entry hall and to the ballroom. The room itself was gorgeous with a soaring frescoed ceiling, a carved marble fireplace, 22-karat gold wall panels, and enough floral arrangements to make me feel like I'd been dropped into a highly stylized version of the rainforest.

The invitation said the party had started at six, and it appeared to be in full swing. Dancers filled the center of the room while on the sides, people stood in small groups, chatting and drinking from crystal glasses or eating from small plates.

I hope I'm not too late already.

My eyes scanned the room, looking for Alex. Thanks to his height, it didn't take long to locate him. He was among the dancers, dressed in a black tuxedo with a snowy white shirt.

He was breathtaking in the formal attire. The woman in his arms was even more so.

With upswept auburn hair and a tall, elegant figure, she was everything I was not. Kristal had said I looked like I was born to this life, but I was merely a cheap imitation.

This woman was the real deal, and it showed from her fabulous floor-length pink ballgown to her manicured nails to her flawless porcelain skin.

His fiancée. It had to be her. They were such a beautiful pair no one would argue with the rightness of their betrothal. And she was probably a *real* princess. It was torture to watch Alex with another woman, watch him smile at her and take her lightly in his arms as they spun around the floor.

For a moment I was tempted to turn around and flee the mansion, making sure *not* to leave a glass slipper behind. But then I thought of Alex's words in his last text to me.

I will always be here... ready to love you and our son.

I wasn't sure how he *could* love me, not after how I'd acted, but I made myself stay. I would find the courage to do the thing I'd sworn never to do again—trust him. Rely on his word.

The song ended, and I moved in Alex's direction. He hadn't spotted me yet. No doubt I was the last person he expected to see in his family's ballroom tonight.

Even if he did see me, he might not recognize me right away after Kristal's magical transformation.

As I neared the spot where Alex and his fiancée stood chatting with several guests, someone stepped into my path.

It was an older man, around my stepmother Julia's age, gray haired and mustached, and like all the other men present, wearing a tuxedo.

Getting a good look at his face, I did a double-take. He had Alex's eyes.

His cleft chin, too. He was considerably shorter than Alex, but this had to be his father.

"Mr. Wessex?" I asked, then quickly corrected myself. "I mean, Your Highness."

The man didn't smile but gave me a quick once-over. "I don't believe you're on the guest list."

His terse remark surprised me. Did the Prince of Aubernesse really recognize every one of his American guests on sight? And then I realized he'd put emphasis on the word "you're" when he'd said it.

He knows who I am.

Maybe I shouldn't have been so amazed, but it simply hadn't occurred to me that Alex's father might have had him followed this week and had his spies report back on the identities of everyone his son interacted with.

I gave him a nervous smile. It was his home after all. I had no wish to make a scene or get into an argument.

"No. I wasn't invited. But I'll only be here a short time. I need to speak with Alex."

The monarch's frown deepened. "*Prince* Alexander is rather busy at the moment."

He cast a glance over his shoulder to where Alex stood side-by-side with the woman his father had handpicked for him. Turning back to me, the prince offered a shallow closed-lip smile.

"Perhaps tomorrow."

"Sir—I mean, Your Highness—I know he's leaving the country tomorrow. Please, I only need a minute of his time."

Determined to speak to Alex, I started to move around the man. The elder Wessex grabbed my wrist in a firm grip.

Speaking quietly, he said, "You don't belong here. You're not royal material. You never were—and neither is your bastard child."

I stopped in mid-motion, my insides freezing solid. I could

barely gather enough breath to form words. "What did you say?"

"I stopped you from entrapping my son years ago. Don't think I can't stop you now."

My head spinning, I reeled in my borrowed pumps.

Alex was right. His father had found out about us years ago—and taken steps to keep us apart. He'd hidden the truth from Alex all this time.

The prince lifted an arm and gestured to someone. A large man in a dark suit and dark shirt started coming toward us from across the room. I was too flabbergasted by Mr. Wessex's words to even worry about the bodyguard.

"You *knew* about me and Alex. You knew he had a child, and you never told him?"

"Who can say who fathered the boy?" the man sneered. "My son and I had words about it today. He's honorable—and gullible—enough that he's willing to accept your word without even demanding proof. I am not so trusting. I will protect my family, no matter what it takes."

Shock prevented me from responding. What kind of a monster would force his son to abandon his *grandson?* If proof was actually what he'd wanted, it would have been easy to obtain.

But that *wasn't* what this man wanted. He wanted Alex to go through with an arranged marriage that would be beneficial to his country, to give up his own needs and desires in favor of duty.

Anger burned in my gut. It was one thing to ask Alex to do all this with full knowledge of his options. It was another to lie to him and manipulate him.

I'd seen plenty of that kind of behavior from my stepmother, first with my father and then with me. In fact, it wouldn't surprise me to learn Julia had conspired with Alex's father to keep us apart years ago.

"If you were *really* concerned with his well-being, you wouldn't have let Alex believe a lie all these years," I said. "You would have let him make his own choices, find his own happiness. What you did wasn't protection. It was manipulation. The only thing you care about protecting is your own interest. Now, if you'll excuse me..."

I tried to push past him. Alex appeared to be moving toward an exit on the other side of the room, and I had to reach him before he left. This might be my last chance to speak with him before he announced his engagement. But as I stepped around the prince, the bodyguard arrived.

"Get rid of her, Frederick," Alex's father muttered.

"Come with me please," the hired muscle said politely. But his grip on my upper arms wasn't polite—it was painful.

Holding me from behind, he began steering me from the ballroom, moving so quickly I was tripping over the hem of my gown trying to keep up.

"Let me go." I tried wrenching away from his grip, but the brute's hands were like iron bands. "Please—you're hurting me."

A new voice entered the conversation—loud and clear. And familiar.

"Frederick. What the devil is going on here?" Alex demanded from somewhere behind me. "Stop this instant. What is happening?"

The bodyguard obeyed, stopping and turning around to face Alex, which meant I was dragged around to face him as well.

Alex's eyes bulged as he recognized me. "Cinda—I thought I heard your voice."

THIRTY-TWO
Root of the Problem

Alex

When I'd noticed my father's bodyguard dragging someone from the ballroom, my first thought had been a paparazzi had snuck in.

Certainly wouldn't have been the first time.

Even when I'd spotted the flash of blue tulle flapping around Frederick's legs, I wasn't overly concerned. There were female paparazzi, and I wouldn't put it past one to try to blend in and disguise herself as a guest in order to get candid photographs of the celebrities and royals in attendance tonight.

But then I'd heard the woman's voice, and I'd literally sprinted across the room to confirm the impossible—*Cinda was here.*

She looked incredible in an elegant dark blue gown, her hair up and studded with sparkling jewels. But it wasn't her appearance that shocked me. It was the fact she was here at all. And that she was apparently being thrown out.

Stepping forward, I reached for her hand and drew her away from Frederick. "What exactly is the meaning of this?"

The bodyguard's heavy brow lowered. "You know her? Your father told me to remove her."

"My *father*?"

I scanned the ballroom, trying to locate him. He was headed our way, along with my mother, sister, and brother. Cam, who'd just arrived, looked a bit rough around the edges as if he'd started the party elsewhere and barely made it here in one piece.

Lowering my head to speak to Cinda, I asked, "Are you okay? Are you hurt?"

She rubbed her bicep. "Not really. I'm fine. I'm sorry. I didn't want to cause a scene. I only wanted to talk to you. I needed to see you before you left tomorrow, to tell you that I was wrong, that I'm sorry for pushing you away... that I don't want you to marry Audrey."

My heart soared with instantaneous joy. The prayers that had filled my sleepless hours last night had apparently been heard. But there were things to be addressed before we could celebrate.

"You didn't cause a scene," I assured her. "My father did. Here, sit down."

Keeping my arm around her, I led Cinda to an ornate padded bench in the mansion's entry hall. "We've a lot to discuss, but first I have to deal with the root of the problem. Don't go anywhere. I'll be right back."

Then I spun around to face my arriving family, feeling like literal smoke was pouring from my ears.

"What is the meaning of this?" I demanded. "The mother of my child comes to speak with me, and you treat her like a criminal?"

"Your child?" Cam's eyes popped wide, and he staggered back a bit. "Wow. A guy goes out on the town one night, and he misses everything."

Jane's red curls slid over one shoulder as she dropped her

chin to pin Cam with a sardonic stare. "You go out *every* night. And sleep all day. If you'd taken any notice of what's been going on around here today, you'd have seen the deRamels storming out in a blaze of fury and know that Alex called off the wedding with Audrey."

"He did?" Cam and Cinda said simultaneously, wearing identical expressions of shock.

"Then who's that?" she asked, pointing at Janey.

With a slight bow and a grin, I said, "May I present my sister, Lady Jane Wessex."

Cam whipped his gaze from Janey's face to mine then over to Cinda. "And who's this?"

"She's the *one*," I said.

Now Cam smiled. "Oh. Nice." He gave Cinda a friendly wave. "Great to finally meet you. Welcome to the royal nuthouse."

Our father was not smiling. "It is *not* nice. It's the farthest thing from nice."

"What's going on?" Mother asked, looking a bit dazed.

Father turned to her. "Your son is attempting to ruin his life and our entire family along with him. He's taken up with the floozy he was seeing the last time he was here in Eastport Bay."

"What floozy?" Mother asked.

Cinda raised her hand. She stood and came over to stand beside me. "That would be me. I'm Cinda Brown."

Father went on, ignoring her entirely. "And now after five years have passed, she's trying to foist her fatherless child on him."

"She's not a floozy," I growled, taking Cinda's hand and pulling her closer to my side. "And AJ is *not* fatherless. *I'm* his father. If you'd even bother to take one look at him instead of making assumptions and accusations, it would be obvious to you."

"I've *seen* the child," Father drawled. "It makes no difference. He is illegitimate. You still have deniability, and we can still arrange a good match for you. If not with Audrey, then someone else."

"A good match is someone you love and trust, someone you actually *know,*" I said.

Father scowled. "After all the trouble I undertook to protect you from your 'youthful indiscretion,' I will not allow this trollop to ruin your life now when you're so close to taking the throne."

"What are you talking about Henry?" Mum looked like she was about to faint from shock and confusion. "What did you do to 'protect" Alex?"

"I was also protecting you—and Cameron and Jane—the entire house of Wessex and our country. When *your son* was last here, he had a summer *fling* and fell victim to this woman's wiles," he explained. "He was determined to be reunited with her. I made an 'arrangement' with the girl's stepmother to... impede his efforts."

"You paid my stepmother to lie to Alex?" Cinda said.

"I simply told her a young man might call her, asking questions, and asked her to say 'no' to all of them. And yes, she was compensated for her cooperation. I assumed you'd benefit financially as well, which was no doubt your goal in striking up a relationship with my son in the first place."

"I had no idea how wealthy your family was, much less that Alex was a royal," Cinda said. "Do you find it so hard to believe someone could love Alex for who he is inside?"

Father scowled. "You knew the beach club was frequented by an exclusive clientele. I'm sure that's why you took a job there."

I'd heard enough. Disgusted, I turned to Cinda. "Come on. Let's get out of here."

"Where are you going?" my mother wailed.

"Home. To be with my family."

"This is your home. Your family is *here*," Father said.

"Not anymore. Not if this is how we treat each other. Not if you refuse to accept the woman I love and our child. You can give the throne to Cameron."

My brother held both hands up in front of him in a defensive posture and shook his head rapidly, saying, "No, no, no, no thanks. Leave me out of this."

"You'll be cut off without a cent," my father warned, his face growing redder by the second. "You'll lose access to the palace and all our other homes around the world."

"I don't care. I'll live here in the States, put that expensive Oxford degree I earned to some use, and get a job."

Walking with Cinda toward the front doors, I called back over my shoulder to my brother and sister, "Janey, Cam, I'll be talking to you." Then I added, "Mum, I'm sure your only grandchild would be happy to meet you when you're ready."

She sniffled and nodded then turned to her husband with a furious glare. "*Do* something to fix this."

Cinda and I were halfway through the front doors when my father's voice rang out, echoing off the marble floors and walls of the entry hall.

"Stop." Then sounding a bit less imperious, he added, "Please."

I drew in a long breath and released it slowly before turning around. "Yes?"

"Please come back inside."

"Is that okay with you?" I asked Cinda. "We can go. I'm dying to hear what you came to say. And I have something to ask you."

She nodded. "It's okay. We can talk here."

When we were back inside the foyer, Father said, "I feel sure this can be worked out. It is imperative you remain as my heir." Tossing a glance at my younger brother, he said, "Cameron is clearly not up to the task."

There was a flash of hurt in Cam's eyes before his usual blasé expression snapped back into place. "That's what I keep telling everyone."

"And..." Father continued. "If you'll agree to stay and carry out the duties of the crown, I will consent to you choosing your own bride... whether it be this girl or someone else."

"There is no one else for me," I stated flatly and felt Cinda squeeze my hand.

My father grimaced. "Very well. We can talk about the rest of it later, paternity tests and such—"

I interrupted. "No. We don't need one."

"It's fine." Cinda patted my arm in a reassuring gesture. "I'm happy to do the test."

Father nodded, pleased with his small victory. "For now... can we all please get back to our guests and try to reclaim some semblance of dignity for our family? I can only imagine the gossip in there."

"You all go ahead," I said. "I'm going to stay here and speak with Cinda privately first."

THIRTY-THREE

The Long and Winding Road

Cinda

Once his family had gone back into the ballroom, Alex invited me to sit on the stairs with him. The train of my blue gown spread over them like a waterfall.

His sincere brown eyes searched mine as he took my hand and spoke softly. “Are you sure you’re okay? I feel terrible. I can’t apologize enough for my father. Mum’s mostly harmless. She didn’t know anything about us.”

I nodded. “I’m fine. I really didn’t mean to cause a scene. I just wanted to speak with you before you left the country. I hated the way we left things. And I was lying when I said I didn’t need you or want you. I want you more than anything I’ve ever wanted in my life. And I need you. AJ needs you, too. I’m so sorry, Alex.”

“I’m the one who’s sorry. None of this would have happened if I’d told you right up front about the arranged marriage. I was afraid it would spook you though. And of course, it did.”

“But you called it off?”

He nodded. “I did.”

"And you called me the woman you love—*in front of* your family."

He smiled. "I did, and I do. The question is... do you?"

"Do I what?"

The smile widened. "I see you're going to make me beg. Do you love me too? Enough to put up with all of..." He gestured around him at the mansion, at the ballroom down the hall. "... this? With a family that's not exactly... normal for the next, oh, sixty years or so?"

I laughed. "Show me a family that *is* normal, and I'll show you some hidden skeletons. I clean out a *lot* of closets, remember?"

"Only if you want to. I *do* want to take care of you and AJ. But if you'd like to keep working, keep running your company, have your own bank accounts, I won't interfere. I know you have a *thing* about relying on people."

That earned a grin from me. "You know... I've been learning lately that some people are pretty darn reliable."

"In that case..."

Alex shifted so he was kneeling on one knee a couple steps below me. Tears sprang to my eyes, and my hand came up to cover my mouth before he'd even reached into the inside pocket of his tuxedo and pulled out the gorgeous sapphire and diamond ring.

"Let's try this again, shall we?" We both laughed, and he went on. "Cinda, you have given me the greatest gifts of my life—true love, a beautiful child, and a second chance. I want to spend the rest of my time here on earth trying to repay you. Will you do me the honor of becoming my wife?"

"Oh Alex. Yes. Yes, I will marry you."

"And I want to have AJ's surname legally changed to Wessex."

"Of course. He's been practicing writing the letter S at school and getting really good at it."

Alex cradled my face in his hands and gave me a kiss worthy of the most romantic fairytale, and I had to admit, that at least in this one case, maybe love *did* conquer all.

When he'd thoroughly ruined Kristal's expert makeup application, I gave Alex a regretful smile.

"I hate to say this… but I have to go."

"What? So soon? It's early. It's not like you're going to turn into a pumpkin or something."

I laughed. "Good one. But Kristal is watching AJ for me, and I promised them both I wouldn't be long."

"I understand. I'll have Patton drive you home. But I'd like to see you and AJ in the morning. Maybe we could go out for breakfast?"

"Why don't you come over and we'll make breakfast together at home?"

Alex leaned in for another brief, sweet kiss. "Together at home. I like the sound of that."

"Me too. You don't happen to be a fan of Star Wars waffles, do you?"

"I'm a fan of anything and everything you want to cook for me."

"Well now, Your Highness, in our house, men cook too," I teased. "And not just canned goods. You should taste AJ's famous worms and dirt pudding."

He beamed at me. "Sounds amazing. I cannot wait."

Alex held my hand as we descended the grand staircase. At the bottom, he gave me a winsome smile. "Are you sure you don't have time for *one* dance? I feel like celebrating."

How was I supposed to resist this guy? "Okay. Just one. Then I really do have to go."

"Excellent. And I know exactly the song I want to dance to."

When we reached the ballroom, he left me momentarily to

speak to the conductor of the orchestra. Returning, he led me to the dance floor and took me in his arms.

As the music started and we began to dance, I tilted my head to the side, catching the opening notes of "The Long and Winding Road."

I threw my head back and laughed then smiled into Alex's shining eyes. "It has been, hasn't it?"

"It has," he agreed. "But we've managed to find our way back to each other. I feel so lucky to have a second chance with you and continue the journey together."

Alex lifted me and twirled me around. When he set me down again, I said, "I'm the lucky one."

"How so?"

"Well, I've just had a handsome prince sweep me off my feet--literally. And I get to spend the rest of my life with the first and only man I've ever loved."

The song ended, and I started to leave the dance floor, but Alex snagged my fingers and pulled me back to the center. "One more minute," he whispered.

The orchestra struck up a new song. "The Bridal Chorus."

"Oh no, Alex, what are you—"

He raised his voice, and the band fell silent. "Excuse me everyone. If I could have your attention, please."

When the crowd chatter quieted, Alex said, "Thank you. And thank you all for being here tonight. You may have heard a rumor that this was to be an engagement party."

He paused, and you could have heard a pin drop.

"It's true." Turning to look at me, he said, "I'd like to present to you the woman who's just agreed to make me the happiest man on earth... the future Mrs. Alexander Wessex and Princess of Aubernesse... Cinda Brown."

Applause and exclamations of delight erupted throughout the ballroom.

Three women standing near the dessert table turned in unison, and their jaws dropped one, two, three.

Then like a submarine cutting through the waters of the Atlantic, they began plowing through the crowd toward us.

Alex lowered his head, speaking to me in a low, private tone. "You're stuck with me now, I'm afraid. I'd like for us to marry as soon as possible. And I want you and AJ to move in with me—here, or in Aubernesse, or anywhere you prefer. It's up to you. This is the smallest of all the Wessex estates, so there's plenty of room. You could even bring along your entire extended family if you like."

Watching Olivia, Traci, and their mother Julia making a beeline for us, I couldn't suppress a bubble of laughter.

"You might want to reconsider that offer, Your Royal Highness. You don't know my stepmother and stepsisters yet."

He followed my gaze, narrowing his eyes. "So this is the 'wicked' stepmother and stepsisters. Do you *want* me to get to know them?"

"Not really. Not tonight. But I guess you have to."

"I'm the prince of Aubernesse," he said. "I don't have to do anything I don't want to do. And as my princess, neither do you."

"Well, in that case, the answer's no. I don't really care to give them a spotlight on our special night. I think I've been far too generous with them already."

Alex grinned. "I couldn't agree more. And I have a surefire way of removing unwanted guests. If you'll allow me?"

When I nodded, he snapped his fingers.

As if they'd materialized out of nowhere, two huge men stepped away from the ballroom walls, making their way to Alex. He directed a subtle hand gesture toward the three eager women and mouthed one word to his bodyguards.

"Paparazzi."

Immediately they turned and seized the three opulently dressed women. "Okay, you're outta here."

The other guard shook his head in disdain. "You paps think you can just go anywhere you want anytime you want. This is a private party."

"Paps?" Julia said as she was dragged from the room. "What are paps? We've done nothing wrong. We know that girl over there. She's my daughter. Get your hands off me you animal."

Olivia protested, "That's my sister over with the prince. My favorite sister,"

"Hey!" Traci slapped her with the invitation she'd just pulled from her evening bag.

The guard holding Traci's arm took the card from her and tossed it over his shoulder.

"An obvious fake. Out you go now. And don't let us see your faces around here again."

Epilogue

Sullivan Reece

One year later

I'd been to my share of parties, but a royal gender reveal party? That was a new one.

The training schedule and travel required for my career as a heavyweight boxer usually made it impossible to go to these sorts of neighborhood celebrations.

Honestly, I'd never had a desire to attend one. But I happened to be home in Eastport Bay this weekend, and my neighbors, Alex and Cinda Wessex, had been nice enough to invite me.

Besides, it would be good for my daughters, Skyla and Claire, to get to know the other neighborhood kids.

I assumed there'd be lots of them there—the invitations *must* have gone out to everyone on Oceanview Avenue because I'd only met the royal couple and their five-year-old son once or twice, and I'd gotten one.

"We need to get a move on, girls," I called out. "The party's already started. Did you pick out some clothes yet?"

Walking through the second floor of the enormous mansion, I searched for my rambunctious young daughters, still feeling like a stranger in my own home though I'd bought it more than a year ago.

For one thing, an interior decorator recommended by my realtor had furnished the place, and it looked more like a magazine spread than an actual home where people lived.

For another, I hadn't spent much time there. Neither had the girls.

But my ex-wife had informed me *that* was about to change. She'd called last week, demanding I pick them up a few days early, as she'd planned a "long girls' weekend" out of town. I'd arrived at her Manhattan apartment to find Skyla's and Claire's bags packed.

All their belongings, not just enough to get them through the weekend.

Never a very involved mother, Anouk said our equitable joint custody arrangement had become "too much" for her and that she needed an extended break. Then she informed me I'd be responsible for the full-time care of our four-year-old and five-year-old daughters over the next three months—the entire summer.

In fact, she'd already had her lawyer draw up the papers to that effect.

I wasn't unhappy about that, but I was a bit shell-shocked. I'd brought the girls here to Eastport Bay, unpacked all their small, assorted pink, sparkly things, and put them into the dresser drawers and oversized closets in their rooms.

Where apparently they were going to remain.

While each of my daughters owned enough miniature designer clothing to fill a Park Avenue boutique, at the moment they were both still wearing their pajamas. At four p.m.

"Claire! Skyla! I'm not kidding now, munchkins. I need you to listen to me and get dressed."

I heard nothing in response but giggles. Fans of hide and seek, the girls were in their glory in the massive house. The hiding spots were limitless.

My patience was not.

If we were going to be full-time residents on this street, I wanted to make a good impression on the neighbors. Strolling into their party an hour late wasn't going to get the job done.

"We'll play hide and seek another time, okay? Right now, Daddy needs you to listen."

Following the giggles, I strode toward the floor-to-ceiling draperies in one of the guest rooms and whipped back one side and then the other. "Gotcha!"

Nothing. I'd always known my little girls were smart as whips. I was learning they were also sneaky and pretty darn fast.

Even with my athleticism and finely tuned reflexes, I had a hard time keeping up with them. They darted around like water bugs and ducked and weaved better than some of my professional sparring partners.

Hearing a happy shriek from somewhere in the hallway, I reversed direction and charged from the guest room—just in time to see the backs of two naturally curly brunette heads disappear into the elevator—their favorite new toy.

I ran for the doors, reaching them just as they closed.

"Girls." I heaved a sigh and checked the lighted panel above the elevator to see where it was headed.

The third-floor light blinked on. They'd gone upstairs where there were even more guest rooms to hide in.

Great.

Slapping my palm against the wall in frustration, I spun

and headed for the stairs, sprinting up them two at a time, hoping to catch the little rascals as they emerged from the elevator.

Unfortunately, I was a minute too late. They were hiding again, and this time there was no tell-tale giggling to clue me as to which direction they'd gone.

Instead of raising my voice, I took a different tact. I lowered it, speaking as softly and sweetly as I could manage as I crept from door to door in the long hallway.

"Okay my princesses, you've had your fun. We've really got to get you dressed now. You don't want to miss the party, do you? There's bound to be lots of fun games, and other kids to play with, and probably a whole lotta fancy cupcakes and stuff. They might even have a pony over there..."

"A pony!"

"Yay!"

The delighted exclamations had come not from the third floor but far below on the first. The girls must have hidden inside the elevator instead of exiting it then taken it down to the ground level.

They tricked me.

Cursing myself for a fool, I sprinted for the staircase again, jogging down it as my frustration level grew.

When I caught up to them, there would have to be consequences... of some kind.

I wasn't sure what exactly. How *did* you convince a four-year-old and a five-year-old to do *anything* they didn't want to do?

At the sound of a door slamming, I froze.

Oh no. Had they left the house? My frustration converted to panic, and my jog turned into a full-speed downstairs run.

Oceanview Avenue, while beautiful, was a busy street, populated at all hours of the day by tourists from around the world, many of whom weren't used to driving on the right side of the road and most of whom had their eyes glued to the gorgeous historic mansions that lined the streets instead of watching where they were going.

What if Skyla and Claire darted out in front of a car?

What if some fool driver was checking his texts instead of looking out for pedestrians?

My heart pounded to the point it was literally moving the front of the uncomfortable button-down dress shirt I'd crammed myself into for the party.

At least the mansion was set far back from the road. My daughters might be quick, but I had much longer legs. Once I got into the open, I could kick it into high gear and catch up to them.

But when I skidded to a stop on the marble floor in the entry hall, I saw the front door was still deadbolted. Obviously, the girls hadn't left that way.

I turned around, calling back through the house. "Claire, baby? Sky? You two still here?"

No answer.

Pulse pounding in my ears, I dashed for the back door, finding that one unlocked. I yanked it open and bolted outside into the lingering late-day sunlight.

My eyes scanned the expansive back yard like radar. They wouldn't head for the far end of the yard, would they?

There *was* an iron fence separating our lawn from the Bluff Walk and the perilous drop to the ocean just beyond it—but Skyla and Claire were so little. Could they squeeze through the spaces between the bars?

There—a flash of pink caught my eye as it slipped through the tall boxwood hedge that separated my property from the Wessex estate.

Apparently my daughters *were* interested in attending the party after all. And had decided to go without me. In their nightgowns.

Fantastic.

They were probably making a mad dash for the cupcake table, where they'd cram the treats into their mouths like they hadn't been fed all day.

That, in combination with the wild, tangled hair and pajamas in late afternoon might be enough to have Child Protective Services ringing my doorbell come this evening.

So much for making a good impression on the neighbors.

Well, there was nothing to do but go after them… and *try* to explain to the Wessexes and their guests why I had absolutely zero control over my children.

Approaching the opening in the hedge, I discovered I was far too large to make it through. I'd have to go around it instead.

I jogged the depth of the back yard, all the way to the fence where the sound of the ocean crashing at the foot of the cliff was loud and clear. I slipped around the outer edge of the prickly natural fence and stopped short at the sight of the party in full swing on the Wessex estate.

This was no regular baby shower. The pool was filled with what looked like hundreds of pink and blue balloons. Several large white tents gave shade to tables decorated with flower arrangements and even more balloons.

Under the tents, groups of adults stood holding small plates and drinks and chatting.

There were far more children than I'd expected. They covered the lawn, playing together, shrieking with laughter. Some were jumping in a bouncy house while others crowded around—yes—a pony in a temporary riding ring.

That was where I headed, surveying the collection of small bodies for my own offspring.

Among those waiting for a ride was the Wessexes' son AJ. I recognized his shiny dark curls.

The boy's parents stood nearby. They were side by side,

holding hands and laughing at their son's antics as he cavorted with two other boys in the pony-ride cue.

Cinda wore a maternity dress and was clearly nearing the end of her pregnancy. Their obvious happiness caused a twinge of envy in my gut.

Sorrow too. Anouk and I had been that happy once—at least I'd thought so.

Aha. I spotted my daughters near the circular fencing, sticking their arms through it and waving at the bored-looking pony, trying to lure him with sprigs of grass.

I picked up my pace, hoping to get to them before they—or I—drew too much attention. There were so many people here. Maybe I could grab the girls and get them back home before anyone noticed us.

Unfortunately, Alex and Cinda did. Both of them waved at me. Sagging, I slowed to a walk. There would be no saving this disaster apparently.

The royal couple offered welcoming smiles as I drew near.

"Mr. Reece," Cinda said warmly. "I'm so glad you and your daughters could make it." She tactfully *didn't* mention the girls' inappropriate attire.

Heat flooded my face as I compared their cartoon-character-covered nightgowns with the other children's fancy party clothes.

What must all the other parents be thinking?

"You've been home a good deal more often lately, haven't you?" Alex asked, extending his hand to shake mine. "It's nice to see you."

"Yes. I have. We have. Thanks. And you can call me Sully. Great party. It's... big."

"Well, the preschool year just ended, and they needed a place to hold a graduation party," Cinda explained. "We thought we'd just combine the occasions. The kids won't care about the gender reveal, of course, but we figured as long as there was a bounce house and plenty of cupcakes, they'd have a good time. They're so cute, aren't they?" she asked with a wrinkle-nosed smile.

Casting another glance at my girls, who I'd just realized were *barefoot* for fuck's sake, I said, "I'm... uh... sorry about how Skyla and Claire look. I've been trying to get them dressed all day, but..."

My explanation died right there. But what? What could I say?

But I have no idea what I'm doing, and my four and five-year-old are completely running the show next door?

I'm drowning, and I don't even know where to find a life preserver?

"Don't be silly. There's no need to apologize. We love PJ days at our house—especially lately." Cinda patted her expansive belly. "It's about all I have left that fits me at this point."

"They're children," Alex said in a reasonable tone. "Who cares what they wear? We're just glad you all came."

"Absolutely. AJ keeps talking about his 'new friends next door' and wanting the girls to come over and play," Cinda said. "I'm not sure whether he's more excited about becoming a big brother... or about having all the other children over today for 'his' party. He certainly won't notice what they're wearing."

"Yes, well, thanks but I'd still like to take them home and get them properly dressed. We'll come back afterward," I promised.

Cinda put a hand on my arm and offered a sympathetic smile. "It's really not necessary. But do whatever makes you comfortable. We won't do the big reveal for about another hour."

"Okay, well, thanks for inviting us. We'll be back soon. And again, I'm sorry."

I stepped away from them toward the pony ring. "Claire. Skyla. I need to talk to you two please."

At the sound of my voice, the girls turned around.

"No," Skyla screeched. "I want to stay at the party."

"Me too." Claire echoed her big sister as usual.

"We'll come back. I promise." In a lower voice I said, "We just need to get some real clothes and shoes on you and brush your hair."

"You do it all wrong," Skyla accused loudly. "It huuuuurts when you brush my hair."

"Me too. It huuuuurts," Claire added in a perfect imitation of her idol's whine.

I looked around uncomfortably at the other party guests, some of whom had definitely heard the charges against me.

Yep. CPS would be at my door tonight for sure.

Putting on her brattiest tone and face, Skyla shouted, "I want *Mommy* to brush my hair," then took off running toward the bouncy house with Claire hot on her little bare heels.

Casting my eyes skyward in a silent prayer, I followed them across the yard. I really did need some divine intervention—I was at my absolute wits' end.

Things had gotten progressively worse over the past few days.

My children's behavior was unacceptable—I knew that. But knowing something and knowing how to *fix* it were two different things entirely.

And I was pretty sure my daughters' acting out was driven largely by their abrupt change in living circumstances—and missing their mom—which broke my heart.

There was nothing I could do about that, but I *did* have to find a more effective way to parent them. I needed to pick up some discipline skills. Fast.

Reaching the bounce house, I stood outside one of the

mesh windows and called to the girls. "We'll go home, change real quick, and come back. But only if you get out of there right now and come with me."

"I. Want. To. Keep. On. Bounce. Ing."

Skyla's words came out individually in time with each jump. Her messy mop of dark hair lifted each time her little feet—which were now dirty and grass-stained—came off the inflated canvas floor.

"I mean it now," I warned. "If you two don't listen to me, I'll..."

What? What would I do? I honestly didn't know what to say.

I looked up again, as if the answer might be written on the fluffy white clouds overhead. Not that I'd gotten a whole lot of response from that direction lately.

Please. Just a little help here...

"Kids that age can be a handful, huh?"

I turned to see the owner of the shy voice that had spoken somewhere near my right shoulder.

And my jaw literally fell open.

There, standing in front of me, was the prettiest human being I'd ever seen in my life.

The young woman appeared to be about three or four years younger than me. Twenty-two? Twenty-three?

"Uh... yeah," I said.

That was about *all* I could say because for the first time in my life—I was utterly speechless. If I didn't know better, I'd have sworn I was looking at a real-life angel.

She wore a simple dress. Yellow and sleeveless, it reached nearly to her knees. Being a fashion model, Anouk would have known what to call the style—I didn't, but whatever it was, it looked great on this girl, hinting at a shapely figure but not flaunting it.

Her long golden hair was pulled back into a ponytail, and she wore no makeup as far as I could tell.

Her big, light brown eyes didn't need it—they were gorgeous.

As far as jewelry, she had on only a pair of tiny diamond studs. No rings.

I checked.

She looked classy and sweet and... *fresh.* Yeah, that was the word. Like sunshine and sea breezes and just-picked citrus fruit.

Wait—*what* had gotten into me? I was nobody's idea of a poet. But I wasn't usually tongue-tied either. Normally, I was great with women.

This one must have thought I was a total imbecile.

"Are you... is one of these kids yours?" I finally managed to ask.

Please say no.

She smiled. "They all are."

I did a double take, looking from the crowded bouncy house to her and back again.

Some of the kids hopping around inside had to be close to eight. And there were so many. How could they possibly all be—

"I'm their teacher—or I was their teacher at some point during the past few years. At the preschool, you know?"

"Oh." Now I got it. "Fantastic. You're a preschool teacher. My youngest is starting preschool in the fall. Where do you teach?"

This time her smile looked a little sad. "I'm just an assistant teacher actually—*was* an assistant. I won't be going back after the summer break."

"Get a new job?" I asked.

Her lips twisted to the side, and she looked away toward the back of the Wessex mansion.

"Something like that."

Okay. She didn't seem to want to talk about it—maybe she got fired? I dropped the subject.

"I'm Sullivan. Reece. Sullivan Reece. I live next door."

She took my offered hand, which I realized with embarrassment had started to sweat. Another first.

"Daddy, watch me," Claire called, jerking my attention back to the bounce house.

She was jumping so vigorously her nightgown flapped above her head, exposing her underwear. Which was inside-out.

At least she was wearing some. If she hadn't been, I might have just given up and turned in my dad-card here and now.

Twisting back toward the woman, I tipped my palms up and shrugged. "I've been trying to get them to go home and put on some clothes and shoes, but I'm striking out. You must think I'm a terrible father."

Her eyes warmed. "Not at all. You wouldn't believe how many kids I've seen show up for school in footy pajamas."

Her lips quirked in the cutest way. "PJ's are comfy. Comfy is good." There was a pause. "Not listening to Daddy is *not* good."

Stepping forward, she ducked to poke her head inside the bounce house's door flaps. "Who wants to play a super-fun game?"

There was a chorus of answers. "Me!"

"I do."

"I want to do a game."

All but the two oldest-looking kids spilled out of the bouncer.

The children, including Skyla and Claire, quieted and watched Angelina as if she might suddenly sprout wings and rise off the ground.

I wasn't at all certain she wouldn't.

Though her voice was soft, it also held an impressive degree of authority. Her command of the children's attention was nothing short of magical.

"Somewhere in this yard, I have hidden—*very* carefully—a treasure," she told them, whispering the last word.

Eyes lit up all around.

"I'll divide you into two teams, and we're going to have a treasure hunt."

There were cheers and shrieks of delight. Angelina quieted them all with nothing but a look and a subtle hand gesture.

"Now to find this treasure, you'll need the clues that I'll pass out to each team—and a good pair of shoes. Is everyone ready? Okay, get your shoes on and let's go."

"Wait," Claire cried, sounding distressed. "I got no shoes."

"You *have* no shoes," Angelina corrected gently. "Did you take them off here at the party?"

"No, they're at our house," Skyla answered.

"Oh dear." Angelina furrowed her brow. "That's a problem."

She appeared to think for a minute, tapping her chin with one finger.

"Maybe we could delay the treasure hunt for *just* a few minutes... if you think you can go and get them on *very* quickly. And treasure hunting will be difficult in your night-gowns, so some regular clothes would be good, too."

"We can be fast," Skyla assured her.

"Fast," Claire repeated, hopping in excitement.

"Okay then, I'll time you and see how fast you are. Ready, set... go!"

The girls took off, speeding toward the narrow hedge opening that led to our back yard.

"You're a miracle worker," I said in amazement, belatedly realizing I should be following my daughters.

Jogging backward, I kept my gaze on the young teacher.

The setting sun behind her caused her blonde hair to glow like a halo around her beautiful face.

"Hey— I never got *your* name," I said.

She waited a beat before answering. "It's Angelina."

All the air left my lungs as if I'd taken a powerful body blow.

As I turned and ran to catch up with my girls, I glanced overhead once more, and this time I pointed up with a laugh and a knowing smile.

"You *were* listening. I owe you one, Big Guy. I definitely owe you one."

* * *

Thank you for reading The Baby and the Blueblood. I hope you loved it!

The Eastport Bay Billionaires series continues with Sully and Angelina's story, **The Baby-whisperer and the Brute, available now.**

And get a free Eastport Bay story when you sign up for my VIP mailing list. I would love to have you on the list— there are fun Tru Tales, freebies, sneak peeks, excerpts and Cupcake of the Week! Sign up at: https://bit.ly/TruTales.

Free Book

If you're interested in reading more in the world of the Eastport Bay Billionaires, my VIP mailing list members get a free novella! Sign up at https://bit.ly/TruTales.

About the Author

Award-winning romance author Tru Taylor writes romantic comedies to make you swoon, smile, and snort with laughter.

She runs on Coke Zero and dark chocolate, lives for lunches with her girlfriends, and drives to the town beach several times a week to watch the sun set over the water.

She loves LOVE and will attempt to turn any show or movie she's watching into a romance whether it is one or not. Star Wars? A romance. Lord of the Rings? Clearly a romance. The Expendables? Okay, well not even Tru can redeem that one.

When she's not writing, Tru enjoys watching movies and reading books with happy endings, spending time with her husband and two kids, and sneaking Hershey's Kisses from the top shelf of the freezer throughout the day. (Top shelf because… two kids. Enough said.)

Tru is the author of the Eastport Bay small town rom com

series and loves living in a small New England town where she's surrounded every day by the beautiful coastal setting you see brought to life in her books.

Want fun email from Tru? Join her Tru Tales mailing list at https://bit.ly/TruTales for true stories of small town romantic comedy, excerpts, sneak peeks, giveaways, and a free novella set in the world of Eastport Bay!

Also by Tru Taylor

THE EASTPORT BAY BILLIONAIRES SERIES

Bookworm and the Beast

Bargain with the Bachelor

The Baby and the Blueblood

The Baby-whisperer and the Brute

The Bombshell and the Bodyguard

Scarlett and the Big Bad Billionaire

The Grumpy Billionaire

The Merry Billionaire

The Sleepless Billionaire (free ebook to all my VIP list members!)

Oxford South Press September 2021

Editor: Judy Roth

Cover designer: Emily Cover Design

www.ingramcontent.com/pod-product-compliance
Lightning Source LLC
Chambersburg PA
CBHW050848190726
48286CB00007B/2276

* 9 7 8 1 9 4 6 1 6 6 3 1 9 *